"You're going to have to jump to me," Jonah said.

He was absurd. "I can't hold on any longer."

"Maddi, look at me." The compulsion in his voice dived deep past skin and muscle, straight into her bones to where she had no choice but to do as he asked. "You didn't come this far to throw it all away now. I know you're tired. I know you're hurting, but you are the strongest, most intelligent and most stubborn woman I've ever known. I want our son to grow up knowing his mother doesn't just put bad guys behind bars but that she stares fear in the face and tells it to go to hell. I want you to be the one he looks up to when he gets older, but to do that, you're going to have to jump to me."

"Okay." She nodded, trying to convince herself more than agreeing to his plan, but she didn't have any other choice. Not if she wanted to get out of here alive.

THE
PROSECUTOR

NICHOLE SEVERN

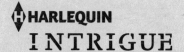

HARLEQUIN
INTRIGUE

To my husband:
for managing to keep me from going insane during
quarantine so I could write this book.

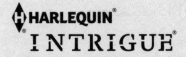

HARLEQUIN®
INTRIGUE®

Recycling programs
for this product may
not exist in your area.

ISBN-13: 978-1-335-40159-5

The Prosecutor

Copyright © 2021 by Natascha Jaffa

This edition published by arrangement with Harlequin Books S.A.

For questions and comments about the quality of this book,
please contact us at CustomerService@Harlequin.com.

Harlequin Enterprises ULC
22 Adelaide St. West, 40th Floor
Toronto, Ontario M5H 4E3, Canada
www.Harlequin.com

Printed in U.S.A.

Nichole Severn writes explosive romantic suspense with strong heroines, heroes who dare challenge them and a hell of a lot of guns. She resides with her very supportive and patient husband, as well as her demon spawn, in Utah. When she's not writing, she's constantly injuring herself running, rock climbing, practicing yoga and snowboarding. She loves hearing from readers through her website, www.nicholesevern.com, and on Twitter, @nicholesevern.

Books by Nichole Severn

Harlequin Intrigue

A Marshal Law Novel

The Fugitive
The Witness
The Prosecutor

Blackhawk Security

Rules in Blackmail
Rules in Rescue
Rules in Deceit
Rules in Defiance
Caught in the Crossfire
The Line of Duty

Midnight Abduction

Visit the Author Profile page at Harlequin.com.

CAST OF CHARACTERS

Jonah Watson—The former FBI bomb technician is forced to put the past behind him to keep the family he's always wanted safe. After already grieving the loss of one child, he's not about to let it happen again despite Madison's best efforts of keeping him at arm's length.

Madison Gray—The deputy district attorney is one of the best prosecutors in Oregon, but with a record like hers, she's made some enemies along the way. Prosecuting the Rip City Bomber case is guaranteed to promote her to district attorney, but she quickly realizes one of those enemies has targeted her and her unborn child.

The Rip City Bomber—Rosalind Eyler is responsible for the detonation of four bombings all over the Portland area and the murder of thirty-two innocent lives. Currently awaiting trial.

Dylan Cove—Fellow deputy US marshal assigned out of Jonah's district office. As a former private investigator, Cove is more than capable of uncovering the truth, but his past mistakes aren't far behind.

Remington "Remi" Barton—Chief deputy US marshal of the Oregon division, and Jonah's superior.

Chapter One

Jury benches had the potential to hide a lot of things.

Old wood protested under his knee as Deputy United States Marshal Jonah Watson crouched to slide his hand under the first bench before the judge and court personnel would take their seats in as little as fifteen minutes. The courthouse was made up of over thirty-nine courtrooms, and he and the other four marshals on his team would search and clear every single one of them.

After seven years of new construction due to age and seismic instability of the old courthouse, the new Multnomah County Central Courthouse had become the nerve center for the Rip City Bomber to meet justice. After triggering four bombs set throughout Portland and murdering thirty-two innocent civilians over the course of the past year, Rosalind Eyler was scheduled to face a jury of her peers to answer for the blood she'd spilled. For the lives she'd destroyed. The sick frenzy of the largest case Oregon District Court had ever seen had already begun. Protestors lined the courthouse perimeter calling for their idol to be found innocent, the media digging for details police had yet to release for the next big story in time for the six o'clock news. There were too many variables in a case like this, too many potential threats.

"I didn't realize you'd be part of the team assigned to clear the courtroom today." And in the center of it all, the all-too-enticing—and all-too-frustrating—senior deputy district attorney prosecuting the case, Madison Gray. Sleek black hair waved down around her shoulders as Jonah pushed to his feet. Her dark green blazer and knee-length skirt accentuated the darker undertones in her skin and highlighted the caramel swirls in her eyes. Sharp features and even sharper heels contributed to her controlling nature and bluntness, but it was the large, soft roundness of her midsection that'd claimed his attention now. Six months pregnant. With his baby. "I specifically requested a special assignment of the east Washington district US marshals to lend us deputies for judicial security."

"Now, why would the district attorney agree to that when he has a former FBI bomb squad technician right here in Portland at his disposal?" He hadn't worked as a unit chief in the hazardous devices school for the Bureau for more than half a decade, but the two years of hands-on training in the middle of a combat zone in Afghanistan had given him all the experience he'd need for the rest of his career. Military ordnance, hand grenades, homemade bombs, thermite. He had the knowledge and the attention to detail required to analyze, investigate and re-create any explosive—improvised or not—he'd come into contact with before joining the marshals service.

The only one he hadn't known how to deal with was the explosion of fire in Madison's gaze when he'd suggested they raise their baby together after she'd told him she was pregnant.

At the time, he'd brushed off her rejection and distance as their one night together all those months ago had turned into something neither of them could walk away from, but five months had gone by, and here she stood, just as adamant. No matter how many times he'd reached out, she'd declined his calls, avoided him in the courthouse hallways and ignored his effort to do the right thing. She wanted to raise this baby on her own and expected him to sign away any rights that came with his role as sperm donor when their baby was born.

She lowered her voice. "You're not supposed to be here."

Jonah crouched to search the next section of the jury bench. The preliminary hearing would start in less than ten minutes, and he hadn't gotten a chance to clear the tables where the deputy prosecutor and the defendant with her counsel would be seated. "What's the matter, Maddi? Afraid the media will see us in the same room together and magically figure out I'm the one who got you pregnant?"

"Why don't you say that a little louder? I wasn't sure the judge heard you in his chambers." Manicured fingernails with a metallic gold polish dug into the freshly stained wood edge of the jury box. "This is the biggest case of my career, Jonah. I can't make any more mistakes. Do you understand?"

A mistake. So that was what she was calling that night they'd been together. Well, it beat not knowing anything at all, he supposed. This conversation had already beaten the record for their longest by two full minutes in the past five months. Jonah couldn't help but revel in the fact that despite all the self-confidence and control she kept in place when she prosecuted a case, he was still able to get a rise out of her. He swept his hand under the last section of the bench and climbed to his feet before dropping out of the jury box. At six foot three, he towered over her small frame, but she held her ground as he closed the distance between them. "Don't worry, Counselor. You just do your job, and I'll do mine. Speaking of which, I need to make sure nothing except my good looks are going to put you and the rest of the people in this courtroom at risk."

Her attention broke as a door off to the left of the judge's bench swung open. Fury slipped from Madison's expression, stiffness entering her neck and jaw, and Jonah turned to face the woman at the center of the Rip City Bomber trial. The defendant herself: Rosalind Eyler. Two sheriff's deputies flanked her on either side, the brightness of her red Multnomah County Corrections uniform stark against their dark green. Equally red hair blended into the fabric around her collar and draped down her back as the steel links between her wrist and ankle restraints rattled with each step toward the defendant's table.

Battle-ready tension thickened the muscles down his spine as Rosalind and her escort shuffled closer. Madison had made it clear the night they'd spent together—the night that'd resulted in new life forged between them—was nothing more than a mistake she'd happily avoid if given a second chance, but that wouldn't stop him from keeping a psychopath out of her orbit.

A sly smile tugged at Rosalind's thin lips, accentuating the heavy-handed spread of freckles over the bridge of her nose. Green eyes, almost the same color as Madison's blazer, brightened. Deep smile lines forged a path from the middle of her face outward. If it weren't for the fact the woman had been caught dead to rights with the components used to build her devices, Rosalind Eyler would've been just another pretty face.

"Madison, how lovely to see you again. I see you've been busy since the last time we spoke." That destructively humorous gaze dipped to Madison's baby bump, and every cell in Jonah's body caught fire with protective fury. Rosalind turned those deceptive eyes on him, and the hairs on the back of his neck stood on end. He'd met plenty of mass killers—terrorists—in his line of work, but none of them could compare to the woman sizing him up right then. No remorse. No guilt. Only pure pleasure. "Congratulations."

Jonah fought the urge to look at Madison for confirmation. There was no way in hell the Rip City Bomber knew he was the father of Madison's child. "Excuse me?"

"Thank you." The deputy district attorney smoothed her hands over the bump, cradling the underside of where their child rested as another man strolled through the door Rosalind had entered the courtroom through and took position at her side.

Pristine suit, lean muscle, slicked hair with a predatory expression cemented in place. Defense attorney. "Ms. Gray, I do hope you're not speaking with my client before today's proceedings. You know as well as I do any communication between the district attorney's office and my client needs to come straight through me."

"Relax, Harvey." Rosalind's attention threatened to burn a hole straight through Jonah's head, refusing to let up before she redirected her half smile toward Madison. "I was congratulating Madison on her pregnancy and giving her my best. I've heard the delivery can be one of the most traumatic events of a woman's life. I do hope she makes it to the finish line in one piece."

Jonah curled his hands into the center of his palms to counter the pressure building in his chest. "What the hell is that supposed to mean?"

A wave of growing voices echoed throughout the room as bailiffs led families, media and law enforcement personnel through the large wooden doors at the back of the courtroom and into the gallery.

"That's my cue." Rosalind stepped carefully in the direction her police escort led her. "Nice to finally meet you, Marshal Watson."

Sheriff's deputies led the bomber to her chair behind the defendant's table and helped her sit down. Rosalind's attorney took the seat beside his client as Madison straightened her shoulders, gave Jonah nothing more than an irritated glance and headed for the prosecution's table.

Court was about to proceed.

Rosalind watched him every step of the way as

Jonah headed for the gallery. That casual smile of hers worked to pierce through the wall he'd built to ignore any distraction that'd keep him from his duty, but the Rip City Bomber couldn't get inside his head. Madison was already taking up too much space in that regard. Taking his seat directly behind the prosecution's table, Jonah automatically stood as the judge entered the courtroom, eyes forward. He'd cleared the courtroom in time for Rosalind Eyler to answer for her crimes, but the fact Madison had taken the case—putting herself and their baby on the front line of defense against a mass murderer—sent a warning straight to his gut.

"You may be seated," the judge said from the raised bench. Four large television screens installed above the grilled sections of wall where air and heat entered came to life as he took his own seat. "The People versus Rosalind Eyler on charges of bombing of public spaces, thirty-two counts of first-degree murder, use of explosives and malicious destruction of property resulting in—"

A cell phone rang off to Jonah's left, near the two television screens taking up the east wall of the courtroom. Slightly muted, probably stuffed down at the bottom of the purse of one of the women toward the end of the pew. Someone hadn't gotten the message to silence their device.

"Whoever brought a phone into my courtroom

had better have a damn good reason." The judge stared out over the gallery in expectation.

Seconds passed, the ringing continued, but no one in the gallery moved to silence the device. Low murmurs swept through the gallery. Three hard strikes of the judge's gavel against solid wood echoed through the spacious room. Jonah craned his head back to get a better sense of where the ringing originated and stood, instincts on high alert. He'd cleared every inch of this courtroom, but something told him nobody in the gallery was moving because the owner of the cell phone wasn't present.

The ringing wasn't coming from someone's bag.

"Order!" The judge struck wood with the gavel again, but Jonah could focus only on the sound seemingly bleeding through the wall.

No. The slight electric echo placed it behind the grilled section of a new HVAC unit crews had installed during the new construction. Understanding hit, and Jonah twisted around. He lunged over the partition of wood separating him from Madison. "Everybody get down!"

A burst of fire and debris thrust him straight into the prosecution's table and knocked the oxygen from his lungs. Blazing heat and pain licked across his neck, the back of his skull and arms as the explosion spread fast and took down anyone in its path. Screams echoed throughout the courtroom. Jonah hit the floor beside the table where Madison had been seconds before.

Then it was quiet.

NOBODY SHOULD'VE KNOWN.

The ringing in her ears momentarily drowned out the panicked rush of movement all around her. A groan escaped her lips as she lifted her head. Senior Deputy District Attorney Madison Gray pressed her palms into the hardwood floor. Fragments of concrete and splintered wood bit into the overheated skin of her hands as time seemed to stretch in a distorted, hazy fluid.

The pristine courtroom where she'd been prepared to present evidence against Rosalind Eyler, the Rip City Bomber, had been replaced by fire, pain and blood. She forced herself to focus on the defendant's table as bystanders struggled to escape the massive space. The sheriff's deputies who'd escorted Rosalind into court hauled their charge from the floor and headed for the holding cells in the room adjacent to the judge's bench. Protocol. They couldn't risk the defendant escaping, but even through the haze of trauma, Madison caught the recognizable smile deepening the bomber's laugh lines on either side of her mouth as Rosalind looked back.

Madison collapsed back to the floor as the strength in her arms gave out. She rolled onto her back, her legs twisted one way, her upper body another. The fire alarm screeched louder each time the back doors swung open into the main corridor of the eighth floor. Frantic movements in her lower abdominals kept her conscious. Her baby. She had to check her baby. The explosion—the bomb—had detonated close enough there was a chance she'd sustained internal bleeding without realizing it. The assignment for this courtroom hadn't been released until this morning. Nobody should've known this would be the location of the Rip City Bomber's preliminary hearing. Nobody should've been able to place an explosive device without the US marshals knowing.

"Jonah." His name strained in her throat. He'd been the closest to the blast. The deputy had lunged over the bar in an attempt to protect her from injury. Only he hadn't been fast enough. He had to be here. He had to be alive. Madison battled to get to all fours. The ringing in her ears ceded, but in its place came a wash of terror and panic. The gallery had been demolished, sobs echoing off the paneled walls. Black scorch marks and flames climbed the bench where the judge had been sitting mere seconds ago. She swiped at a line of warm liquid running down the side of her face, hand shaking. Blood.

And there on the other side of the table, the father of her child. Unconscious.

Madison licked dust-covered lips as she stretched one hand forward, then brought her knee up to follow. On hands and knees, she crawled around the prosecution's table until she could slide her fingers into his palm. "Jonah, get up."

He jerked into consciousness, his hand clasping hard around hers. Black-singed ends of hair curled at the base of his neck and around his full beard of light brown thickness. Alarm flashed in iridescent blue eyes at the sight of the aftermath still unfolding around them. Thick ropes of muscle hardened as he pushed upright. "Madison."

"I'm here." Relief coursed through her. He was alive. As far as she could tell, he hadn't been too injured. She tugged her hand from his, falling back onto one hip, and held on to the solid curve of her baby bump. She couldn't breathe, couldn't think. Someone had triggered an explosion inside the very same courtroom where Rosalind Eyler was scheduled to answer for what she'd done, but Madison didn't have time to investigate why, how or when. "I… The baby."

His gaze immediately dropped to her lower abdominals. He reached for her in the same moment and, without hesitation or consideration for any injuries he might've sustained from the explosion, scooped her into his arms. It didn't matter what'd happened between them, how many times she'd declined his calls or how often she'd gone out of her way to avoid him in their professional interactions. Past experience and his case history said she could count on him to care about this baby. Debris crunched under his boots as he maneuvered around the unrecognizable bench he'd been sitting on before the blast. "I'm going to get you out of here. Hang on to me."

Reality sped into focus as the fire alarm shrieked in her ears. Heels clicked on polished tile behind them as Jonah pushed through the damaged courtroom doors and into the corridor. Courthouse security shouted from the bank of elevators and directed them toward the stairs. The elevators had gone into automatic lockdown. Rubble slid across the floor and slammed into the baseboards as victims of the explosion stumbled from the courtroom. The dark green color of her skirt-suit had turned an ash gray, tiny holes pockmarking the hem on one side. This was supposed to be her big case, the one that'd put her in line for the district attorney. This was the case that would've proved she'd risen above her past, but now her chance was gone. Disintegrated in the leftover ashes of that tinderbox.

Emergency personnel raced toward them from the stairs.

"Issue an evacuation of this building! I want all the top floors cleared as fast as possible. That bomb could've damaged the structural integrity of the entire courthouse." Jonah gave orders without slowing. The command in his voice neutralized the panic clawing up her throat. This was what he did for a living. This was what the FBI had trained Jonah for domestically and in Afghanistan for two years. When the entire world threatened to collapse around her, he'd fallen directly into his element to be the voice of calm and reason, and she couldn't help but latch onto that strength and try to take some it for herself. "I counted twenty-six injured, eight dead and no sign of the judge or the bailiff."

Eight dead? So many lives destroyed. How could this have happened? Why?

The answer burned on the tip of her tongue as Jonah ran toward the stairs. The Rip City Bomber. Rosalind Eyler was connected somehow, and Madison would prove it. As soon as the EMTs cleared her and the baby's health, she'd get in touch with the district attorney. She'd get the bomb squad to analyze the scene and bring new charges against the defendant to make sure Rosalind never saw the outside of a prison cell for the rest of her life. The same sentence Madison's father should've met all those years ago.

New determination chased back the terror that'd taken control.

"Put me down." Madison pressed her palm into Jonah's chest, the fast-paced pounding of his heart in rhythm with hers. She had enough strength to get herself downstairs and checked by one of the arriving EMTs. He needed to be here. He needed to help as many people as he could, and she could take care of herself. "I can walk from here."

"That bomb detonated less than fifteen feet from where you were sitting, Maddi." He easily kept pace down seven floors of courthouse stairs with her added weight. The scent of smoke and something she couldn't identify clung to the deep brown corduroy of his jacket. Nothing like the rich cinnamon spice she'd missed these past few months. "There's no way in hell I'm giving you the chance to run before I make sure you and my baby are okay for myself."

My baby. Those two words sunk like a rock in her stomach. Despite the fact he was indeed the father of the life growing inside her, she'd committed to raising this child on her own after the birth—physically, financially and emotionally. Just because they'd made a baby together didn't mean she needed to rely on him for help or security. But because he'd defended his argument to carry her with the safety of her and the baby in mind, she couldn't offer a rebuttal without throwing her priorities into question. She cared about this baby. There was no argument to be had, but his concern worked under her skin and scratched at her independence. She'd gotten this far on her own, and she sure as hell wasn't one of his damsels in distress to be saved.

Cold Portland air shocked every inch of her exposed skin as Jonah kicked open the lobby doors and maneuvered her through. Fire and police vehicles condensed onto the scene as panicked civilians crowded the perimeter the Portland Police Bureau had established and pointed up the side of the building. Madison followed their gazes. Dread pooled at the base of her spine where Jonah's hand supported her. Black smoke and bright flames escaped what she could see of the massive hole the bomb had created, and air crushed from her lungs.

Fifteen feet. She'd been only fifteen feet away from the blast and somehow survived an explosion that'd ripped an entire hole in the side of the Multnomah County Central Courthouse building. Gravity increased its hold on her body as the reality of that thought bled into focus. This didn't make sense. If the bomb had been strong enough and positioned well enough to blow a hole through several feet of concrete and steel, how had she walked away and eight others hadn't?

Jonah's grip strengthened around her back and alongside her thigh as he rushed her to the closest ambulance. "I have a survivor. Deputy District Attorney Madison Gray, age thirty-three, multiple head lacerations, possible internal bleeding and six months pregnant. You need to make sure she and the baby are okay."

Red and blue patrol lights blurred in her vision as he hauled her into the back of the ambulance. Within seconds, emergency staff had a blood pressure cuff strapped around her arm and an oxygen mask in place. Her breathing echoed back to her through the mask. Her heart rate spiked as the facts of the explosion lined up in her head, but the heaviness of Jonah's gaze anchored her enough to drown the uncertainty clawing up her throat.

"You're going to be okay. I promise." Jonah wrapped a calloused hand in hers at the side of the gurney. Instant warmth shot through her at that single touch, the same warmth that'd led to her getting pregnant by him in the first place, and the world tilted on its axis. From the added oxygen or from him, she didn't know. "I'm not going anywhere."

Static interrupted the sense of peace his confidence instilled deep in her bones. A female voice penetrated the small bubble he'd somehow created between them and the violent chaos outside the ambulance walls. "Deputy Watson, I need you to meet me on channel two."

Extracting his hand from hers, Jonah peeled the radio strapped to his Kevlar vest from his chest and turned the dial. Compelling blue eyes shifted out the back of the ambulance, and in an instant, the spell was broken. The one that had the ability to convince her to let him get past her guard again, that she could trust his intentions. "Glad to hear you survived, Chief. What do you have?"

Remington Barton, Jonah's deputy chief. Madison had met the woman only a couple of times during judicial security assignments and testimony proceedings, but each encounter had been ingrained in Madison's memory. The former New Castle County sheriff held her own in a job dominated by the opposite sex and rarely backed down without a fight. For her deputies, for her witnesses and anyone else lucky enough to be brought under her protection. "An anonymous source has just taken credit for the bombing."

Jonah compressed the push-to-talk button. "And?"

The deputy chief didn't miss a beat. "The call confirmed Deputy District Attorney Madison Gray as the bomber's target."

Chapter Two

I do hope she makes it to the finish line in one piece.

Rosalind Eyler's words spoken mere minutes before the explosion ripped apart that courtroom echoed on repeat in his head as Jonah lunged out the back of the ambulance. The radio's casing nearly buckled under his grip as he studied the perimeter of onlookers and civilians beyond the caution tape marking the scene.

"Jonah." His name pierced through the oxygen mask covering Madison's nose and mouth, drawing his attention back to her stretched out on the gurney. Lines of dirt and debris sharpened the angles of her face. Her hair, usually smooth and without a single strand out of place, was frizzed and more textured than a mere twenty minutes ago.

The mother of his child was the target of a bomber.

The Rip City Bomber case was the biggest the

state of Oregon had ever seen in domestic terrorism. Every detail, including the fact Madison had
been assigned as the lead prosecutor, had been
made public, but there were details the district attorney's office hadn't released to the media. The
device he'd heard had been wired with a cell phone
to trigger the detonation. Whoever'd set that bomb
had to know the layout of the courtroom, where
the prosecution's table would be positioned and
the minute the preliminary hearing had started in
order to achieve full destruction. The only way
the bomber would've known the exact moment to
detonate was if they'd been close enough to ensure
their target was in range.

Only something had gone wrong.

The blast had mainly diverted to the outer wall
of the building. Jonah memorized every face in the
crowd, every officer and EMT on the scene. The
bomber had failed in getting to Madison, which
meant there was a chance they'd try again.

His blood pressure rocketed into dangerous territory. He had to get her out of here. For the sake of
her life, their baby's life. Jonah closed the distance
between him and the back of the ambulance, his
right shoulder blade screaming with the slightest
jerk of his arm. The sight of one of the paramed-
ics with his hand pressing into the exposed, flawless curve of Madison's belly tugged at something

under Jonah's rib cage. He strapped his radio back onto his Kevlar vest. "How is she?"

"She's stable. No sign of internal bleeding or fetal distress," the EMT said, "but we should still get her to the hospital to do an ultrasound and make sure mother and baby are in the clear."

"Can she be moved to a different location?" he asked.

"Jonah, no." Madison pushed upright, the set of that perfect mouth rigid as though she could read his mind. "I'm not going into protective custody. I need to be here. I need to finish what I started."

Every second she was out in the open was another chance the bomber had of taking away everything Jonah had fought to protect. Madison had made it clear she intended to raise this baby on her own when she'd walked away all those months ago, but that wouldn't stop him from doing whatever he had to do in order to keep her and their child alive. The EMT hadn't answered. "I said, can she be moved?"

"Yes." The emergency technician backed himself into the side door of his rig, eyes wide. "Her vitals are fine, but, Marshal Watson, you're bleeding. We should take a look at that wound on the back of your shoulder."

"That's the least of my problems right now." Stepping up into the back of the ambulance, he pressed his hand beneath Madison's elbow and urged her to get to her feet. "Deputy District Attorney Gray, you are officially under US Marshal protection for the duration of the investigation into today's attack, and I'm getting you out of here."

"Like hell you are." She wrenched her arm out of his hold, that caramel-brown gaze molten. Every ounce of the independent, self-confident and controlled woman he'd been battling with the past few months rose to the surface as though he were one of the defendants she prosecuted in the courtroom. She stood on her own. "Rosalind Eyler killed thirty-two people in the past year. Thirty-two people who won't ever get to see their families again, and I'm the only one who can make sure she pays for that. If I'm going anywhere, it's back to get the bomb squad here to prove to the DA we should add this attack to the charges I'm bringing against her." She maneuvered past him to step down from the ambulance. "I've got a job to do, and there's nothing you can do to stop me."

Moving fast, Jonah pulled his handcuffs from the pocket at the back of his vest and wrapped one cuff around her hand clutched to the ambulance door. He secured the other end around his own wrist as she turned on him, then pulled her deeper into the back of the rig. Tugging her wrist up between them, he stepped into her. "You've made it perfectly clear you want nothing to do with me these past five months, Maddi, and there's

not a damn thing I can do about that. But whoever targeted you knows who you are. They know
where you work, where you live, what car you
drive, who your friends are, that you're six months
pregnant and your daily routine. They've watched
every public interview you've given and figured
out how desperate you are to prove yourself on
this case. They'll know your next move and the
one after that, and they're going to find out they
failed in killing you today. Unless you come with
me right now, they're going to try again." He lowered his voice low enough to keep his next words
between them. "So I'll make it clear to you now,
Counselor. You might think your job is so important to you that you would risk our baby's life, but
I'm not willing to take that chance."

He'd already lost too much.

The small muscles on either side of her throat
flexed as she swallowed. Hardness in her expression shallowed. Seconds passed, maybe a minute.
"How do you know? How do you know whoever's
behind this has gone to that much trouble to dig
into my life?"

"Because that's exactly what I would've done."
He'd investigated enough improvised explosive devices to determine the state of mind of the bombers
behind them over the years. Ranging from Middle
East combat zones where the devices were meant
to cause as much damage as possible for a cause,

to homegrown terrorists sending a message as he'd assisted state and local bomb techs, Jonah knew without a doubt whoever'd targeted Madison had made this personal. This attack hadn't been about a cause or killing as many people as possible. It'd been about one person: Madison. As much as he wanted to suit up and be part of the bomb technician team that would be assigned to assess the threat in the rest of the building, he needed to be here. For her. He wasn't FBI anymore. He was a US marshal, and his judicial security had just become a witness protection assignment. "I need you to trust me. If you want to get out of this alive, if you want our baby to make it out of this alive, you're going to have to do exactly as I say."

Her shoulders rose and fell with exaggerated breath. She nodded.

"Good. Take your heels off and hand over your phone. We're headed for my SUV parked around the corner. The bomber most likely knows what kind of car you drive. Move fast but don't run, stay low and keep hold of my hand at all times." He dug the handcuff keys from his pocket and twisted the cuff off his wrist, then hers. A sudden high-pitch protest of Velcro ripping free filled the back of the ambulance as he hefted his Kevlar body armor over his head and maneuvered the thick vest onto her shoulders. He pulled the fasteners tighter at her sides. "Use me as a shield if you have to."

Madison removed her shoes, long fingers wrapped around the heels in one hand, then unpocketed her phone from her deep green blazer and handed it over. "You think whoever set off that bomb is here? You think he's watching me?"

"I'd rather take every precaution and be wrong, than take none and have the bastard surprise us. IEDs come in a lot of shapes, sizes and forms, and there's no way to know if the bomber has set any other devices until the bomb squad is on scene and can clear this entire block." Powering down her phone, he intertwined his hand in hers. "We have no idea who we're dealing with, Maddi, and until we do, I need to get you off the grid and into hiding. That means no phone calls, no email, no messages or contact with your friends, family and coworkers. As of this moment, you're under the protection of the United States Marshals Service. It's the only way I know to keep you safe."

Madison's gaze shot to his as she clasped his hand. "Okay, but there better be dill pickle chips when we get wherever you're taking me."

"I think I can manage that." Jonah tightened his hand around hers and fell into the mindset he reserved for high-risk operations. Any time he'd approached a suspicious package, backpack, a pressure cooker on the side of the street or been assigned to gather evidence after an explosion outside American bases across the ocean, nothing mattered but the objective. In Afghanistan, it'd been to collect as many pieces of evidence as he could and re-create the device in a controlled environment to figure out how it functioned. Right now, it was getting Madison to safety. Nothing else could get in the way. "Three. Two. One."

They stepped from the back of the ambulance and headed straight for the perimeter of tape the Portland Police Bureau had secured around the scene. She struggled to keep up with his long strides as he wound her through the crowd of spectators and police. "Not too fast. Don't draw attention to yourself."

"I think the burn marks in my dress will do that for me." She kept her head down and a tight grip on her heels, but she was right. They wouldn't be able to hide the fact they were covered in ash and blood for long. The faster they left the area, the better.

"You're doing fine." He checked back over his shoulder mere feet from the corner of the courthouse, focused on the familiar car parked four spaces down. Madison's. Twenty more feet and they'd be in range of his SUV. "Just keep—"

The second explosion hurled a fireball and blast wave straight into the sky between buildings. Jonah pulled her into him, covering her with his own body as much as he could as glass and small chunks of cement rained down on top of them. Fire engulfed the parked vehicle they'd passed mere seconds before, the same car he'd recognized a split second before it'd gone up in flames. Dust and debris clouded the air. Another round of panic echoed around them as he straightened, Madison's gaze fixed on the same vehicle. Hot air burned down his throat and into his lungs. "I see you drove to work today."

"THEY PUT A bomb in my car." Madison was barely able to say the words. Who would do this to her? Who would target her? Who would try to kill her? The soft vibration of tires against asphalt did nothing to calm the chaos churning through her. She held on to her heels a bit tighter than necessary as Jonah drove them over the Morrison Bridge. Deep blue water spread out on either side of them, beautiful and entrancing, but she couldn't focus on that right now. Couldn't focus on anything other than the fact if he hadn't taken her into protective custody, she would've gotten in that car to drive to her office. She would've died trying to prove Rosalind Eyler was behind the attack in the courthouse. "If they'd planned on the first device to kill me, why set another one in my car?"

"Backup plan," he said. "Must've been tracking you—visually or electronically—and figured out you'd survived the first explosion. They had the second one waiting for you, to finish the job.

Only they hadn't counted on me taking you to my vehicle instead."

None of this made any sense. She was a deputy district attorney. She couldn't deny the cases she'd prosecuted had made enemies over the years, but the line was ten times longer for her boss. Although, trying the Rip City Bomber case as she'd nearly died from a bomb in the same courtroom as Rosalind Eyler was too much of a coincidence to ignore. The only question still out of reach was motive. If she found the motive behind the attack, she could narrow down the suspect, whether that was Rosalind herself, someone close to the bomber, possibly a family member of one of the victims. Once she had a motive, she could secure her future. For her and her baby.

"Thank you for getting me out of the building. There were a lot of other people that needed help, but you made sure I made it to the ambulance." But it hadn't been about her. Not really. She slipped her hand over her growing baby bump. *You might think your job is so important to you that you would risk our baby's life, but I'm not willing to take that chance.* Jonah's accusation twisted the knife in her heart deeper. Because when she'd found out she was pregnant from their one night together, she'd instantly thought of her career. Of how a baby would change the plans she'd set for herself over the next five, ten, twenty years.

How this small, precious life she'd become accustomed to over the past few months would derail her chances of being elected to district attorney down the line. She hadn't thought of the impact her decision would have on the child they'd created together, hadn't even thought of Jonah or what he might want. "You were wrong before. I do care about this baby. You have no idea how much. I would never put its life at risk for the chance to get ahead in my job."

Those hypnotic blue eyes she'd fallen prey to over the years remained fixed out the windshield. He hadn't told her where he planned to take her, hadn't spoken much at all unless it'd been about the scene they'd left behind, and the air between them grew thick. His grip slid down the steering wheel as they crossed to the other side of the bridge. "You're right. I don't know how much you care. You've been keeping me at arm's length ever since I told you I wanted to be involved, that I intended for us to parent this baby together."

The knot of guilt that'd formed the moment she'd said those words all those months ago spread like a wildfire. She'd done this to them. She'd taken their friendship—one built on years of him escorting her to and from the courthouse, playful banter and mutual attraction—to the next level, then turned her back on him the instant she'd seen those two blue lines on the pregnancy test. Not only had she severed the connection between them as lovers, but she'd destroyed their relationship as friends, and he deserved better. He deserved to know why. "It's not about you, Jonah. It's... It's about not being forced to rely on someone other than myself. Not being trapped in a situation neither of us can escape from."

"And you believe because we'll be raising this baby together that you'll be bound to me for the rest of our lives?" He directed the SUV onto the 26, taking them east toward Mount Hood. Snowcaps hid the sharp curve of the peak she'd become familiar with since relocating to Portland five years ago, straight out of Berkeley Law, but that still gave a deep sense of wonder and order she craved. "It took two people to make that baby, Madison. Stands to reason it'd take two people to raise it."

Madison. Not Maddi. That one simple change managed to disrupt the emotional calm she'd been trying to hold on to since Jonah had placed himself between the bomb in the courtroom and her. The logical part of her brain said he'd only been protecting his offspring that happened to be inside her body. But the other part of her, the part that missed what they'd had together before she'd learned of the pregnancy, was working hard to convince her he still cared about her. That he'd gone out of his way to make sure she walked out of that courtroom alive. Not because of the baby but because he missed what they'd had, too. "Twenty-three percent of all kids in the country are raised in single-parent homes. Statistically, they might not have the same advantages as a two-parent home, but I make enough money to support us, especially if I'm elected to DA when my boss steps down in a few months. The Rip City Bomber is a career-changing case guaranteed to position me as a front-runner for his job."

"I know what your job entails. I'm the one who escorted you to and from the courthouse every day until you asked for another marshal to take over my assignment. Early mornings, late nights, mountains of takeout and long hours." The city bled to countryside the farther he took them out of the city. "Do you think it's going to get any better when you're the district attorney? Are you even going to be able to take time off to recover from the birth?"

"I've already hired someone to help me when the baby comes." She stared out the passenger side window. It wouldn't get easier. If anything, the long hours and exhaustion would get worse, and she'd still have an infant to care for when she came home. Her child would have to be with a caretaker throughout the day, but the alternative wasn't an option. Not after she'd witnessed what her mother had been through all those years. "I'm not saying it'll be easy, but it's still my decision to make."

His exhale filled the silence between them. "You're right, and I'll respect that decision as much as I don't see the reasoning behind it, but you need to know you don't have to do this alone."

Yes, she did.

"My father was abusive. He drank. He got addicted to drugs, and when he'd come off his high, he'd take it out on my mother." Madison stared out the window. She couldn't remember the last time she'd taken the opportunity to get out of the city. Tall, green pines and light-faced rock streamed past the window, but she couldn't focus on the beauty of any of it. "He could barely hold down a job, but he was adamant she wasn't allowed to work. He needed to know where she was, who she was talking to and what she was doing at all times, leaving us with barely enough to get by or have food on the table. And that's the way he wanted it."

"You never talked about your family when I asked," he said.

"I'm not ashamed of the way I grew up. I'm the woman I am because of what I went through. It took a lot of self-awareness and healing for me to realize it, but I'm proud of the fact I worked harder than anyone else in my class. I made sure I had the opportunity to get out of there the moment I graduated high school by keeping my grade point average the highest of all my classmates, applying for scholarships, working as many jobs as I could. I put everything into getting into law school because I didn't want to be trapped in that life. With him. Like she was."

"Your mother." His voice dropped low, unleashing a flood of renewed illusions that taking her into protective custody was something more than protecting his child.

"He controlled every aspect of her life. He made the rules. He made sure she couldn't leave no matter how bad it got. She tried. Some of my clearest memories are her waking me up in the middle of the night, my bags already packed. We'd spend a night here, a night there, at some crummy hotel in the city thanks to a few bucks one of her friends had thrown our way, but the money always ran out. And she'd go back to him." Madison forced herself to take a deep breath. She had to detach from the pain and move forward more analytically. She'd made a mistake in letting herself imagine there could be more between her and Jonah, and now they'd slipped into an intimacy neither of them could recover from. "I never planned on this pregnancy, Jonah, but the thought of being tied to the father of my child scares me. I don't want to end up like my mother. I don't want to be helpless and controlled. I don't want to give anyone the opportunity to have that power over me. Raising this baby on my own is the only way I can see to make sure that never happens."

The tendons along his neck bunched, revealing the power and strength beneath the thin layer of his T-shirt, as he slowed the SUV. Shadows engulfed them on either side as they took the next unpaved road deeper into the wilderness but within minutes vanished. A large, majestic cabin sat off to the left of a wide clearing surrounded by the tallest trees she'd ever seen. Beautiful landscaping of shrubbery hugged up against the deck and well-maintained grounds. Countless windows and a skylight reflected warm spring sun, inviting and golden. Sharp angles and beautiful wood blended perfectly with the surrounding forest, and an instant feeling of peace washed through her. It was beautiful. The SUV slowed to a stop, and she reached for the door handle.

"I'm sorry all that happened to you growing up, Maddi. I can't imagine how scared you must've been living in that house, but I'm not your father." Jonah shouldered out of the SUV, hand on the door. "The only thing I care about is the safety and happiness of you and that baby. I just wish you'd give me the chance to prove it."

Chapter Three

This wasn't how it was supposed to be.

Taking Madison into protective custody should've been easy. She'd been in danger, and he had the skills to get her out of it. Simple as that. Whatever'd happened between them wasn't supposed to get in the way of their current arrangement, but as she'd revealed the past she'd been keeping to herself all these years, his protective instincts had taken control. He wasn't her father. He'd never go out of his way to control her or their child, never intimidate her, hurt her or trap her in an unbearable situation. Having her walk away from what'd he'd considered the most intense and fulfilling friendship of his life had ripped him apart, but she didn't want the past to repeat itself. Didn't want their child caught in the middle of a toxic environment if things between them hadn't worked out, and he had to respect her decision.

Jonah unloaded his supply bag from the back

of the SUV, then paused before hiking up the small incline toward the front door of the cabin, his shoulder on fire. But he couldn't accept never seeing his child once he or she was born. Never having the opportunity to hold the life they'd created together, to be there for their first word, first step, first day of school. To sing their baby to sleep or watch them drift off in his arms. He'd missed out on a lot of that when his son, Noah, had been born. He'd been stationed overseas with the FBI, and when he'd returned home, it'd been too late. "This way."

"If I would've known this place existed the night we slept together, I would've insisted we come here instead of going back to my house." Heels still clutched in one hand, Madison studied the tall rise of the front of the cabin with floor-to-ceiling windows reflecting fading sunlight back into her face. Dried ash and blood clung to flawless warm-colored skin, the rips in her pantyhose revealing scrapes and a longer laceration across her shin, but right then, she was still one of the most enthralling women he'd ever met. "It's beautiful. Quiet."

A laugh escaped up his throat. "Comes with an indoor hot tub, too."

"Get out of my way. My feet are killing me." She marched past him, one hand beneath her growing belly, the other swinging her heels for momentum up the incline. Lean muscle flexed along the backs of her legs as she took the stairs up to the front door. Pushing inside, she slowed slightly beyond the entrance. "I should've agreed to protective custody sooner."

"It's mine." The air-conditioning cooled the stinging skin along his neck as he closed the door behind them. After setting his duffel bag on the bench that made up part of the mudroom, he armed the alarm panel just inside the door. Amazement smoothed the hard set of her mouth, and he couldn't help but memorize the effect. "I bought it before the Bureau assigned me to Afghanistan. Doesn't get much use nowadays since I've relocated closer to the city, but you'll be safe here. Top-of-the-line security system installed by the premier security company in the country, remote location and no connection to you, the DA's office or the marshals service. Whoever's targeted you won't be able to find you here."

"May I...?" She motioned into the main living space.

"Be my guest." He followed in her path as she took in the twenty-foot ceilings, the wood-burning stove he'd gated off to keep small fingers from getting burned. Watched as she ran her fingers over individual books stacked on the shelf off to their left. A light-colored wood made up the grand staircase leading up to the bedrooms over a kitchen built with the same stain on the cabinets and island. Skylights cast pink rays across the prosecutor's face, highlighted the darkness of her hair. He could still see this place as the family home he'd meant it to be when he'd purchased it, but knowing now what he did about Madison's past, he wasn't sure that'd ever be a possibility. "There are four empty bedrooms upstairs for you to choose from, but the main is the only one that has an en suite bathroom. You should have everything you need in there if you want to clean up."

She turned to face him, running her palms down her hips. "I don't have any fresh clothes."

"I keep some shirts and sweats in the closet in case I leave directly from work to come up here. You're welcome to help yourself to anything you need while I put together something for us to eat." He headed for the pantry, making a mental list of the provisions he had on hand. "I don't have dill pickle chips, but I can have another deputy pick up some bags and pack you a few items from your house—"

"Jonah, what are you doing?" Soft footsteps reached his ears a split second before long, delicate fingers wrapped around his arm. She dropped her heels at her feet and turned him toward her. "How long were you going to stand there and bleed until you said something?"

"In case you didn't notice, I had more important things to worry about at the time." In truth, he'd planned on taking a look at the wound in the smaller bathroom while she cleaned up in the main. No need to stress her or the baby out more than she already was, but it was obvious he wasn't going to be able to hide it from her any longer. He let her move him toward the large circular dining table where he'd imagined hosting family dinners and holidays and took a seat. The pain in his shoulder reignited with white fire around the wound. The shrapnel had penetrated past clothing and skin, but not enough time had passed to put him in danger of going into shock.

"For as much as you lecture me about not raising this baby alone, you sure don't apply the same concern to yourself." Her hand slipped from his arm, and he felt the distance in a gut-wrenching kind of way. "Where's your first aid kit?"

"Under the sink." He motioned his chin toward the kitchen island.

She didn't wait for permission, turning her back on him to disappear behind the cabinet, but even that moment of not having her in his sight line raised heated awareness of her. Within seconds, the caramel-colored eyes he'd envisioned their baby to inherit settled on him as she approached with the white-and-red kit in her hand. "Take off the shirt."

The request hit him square in the chest. "Don't

have to sound so disappointed about it. I seem to remember there was a time you couldn't wait for me to get my shirt off."

A small laugh bubbled past her lips, and the world threatened to slip right out from under him. He'd missed that laugh. Missed her, if he was being perfectly honest with himself. Jonah peeled his shirt over his head, careful of the small piece of metal that'd torn through the muscle in his shoulder. The days he'd been assigned to escort her to and from the courthouse were some of the memories that stuck in his mind the longest. He'd been at her side not only as part of his protection detail, but also because he'd genuinely gotten comfortable there. He'd looked forward to hearing her talk about her day, wanted every detail she could reveal about the cases she was working on and strived to learn more about her. Time had no meaning when they'd been in the car together, and if he'd realized one morning she'd request another marshal to take over his detail, he would've gone out of his way to memorize every detail of those long hours he'd taken for granted.

"Yeah, well, don't get any ideas of something like that happening again." Madison pressed her thumb near the wound, and he sucked a cold hiss of air through his teeth to counter the sharp attack of pain. "Sorry. I'm not a doctor. I'm not exactly sure how to do this."

Better to feel the pain than feel nothing at all. He had to remember that. "Sanitize your hands with the rubbing alcohol pads in the kit and clean around the wound as best you can. You'll have to remove the shrapnel with the tweezers."

She did as instructed. Calm. Collected. Controlled. Everything he wasn't as he recalled how the damn piece of metal had gotten there in the first place. She was alive. She was safe. She was a target, and he wasn't sure how he was supposed to feel about that. He'd already lost too much. He couldn't lose her, too. A metallic ping registered off the surface of the table. "It's out. Now what?"

"Now you hand me the gauze and tape and rest while I check the security system and make us some lunch." He stood, overshadowing her by more than a foot and a hundred pounds. Despite their differences in size, she'd taken on far more dangerous predators in her line of work without a single crack in that confident expression. Predators like the Rip City Bomber. Madison Gray had risen above a past determined to break her in every way. As long as he'd known her, there was no blockade she couldn't get through, and damn, if he didn't admire her for it.

"Suit yourself." She handed over the roll of tape and gauze and turned away from him toward the grand staircase leading up to the second level. Halfway between the dining room table and the stairs, she slowed. Hesitation bled into her stride. Sections of damaged hair slid across her back as she turned to face him. "You put yourself between me and that device in the courtroom, knowing you'd take the brunt of the blast if it hadn't diverted to the outer wall of the building. Was that because you were trying to protect me? Or protect the baby?"

Bits and pieces of memory flashed across his mind. Holding his baby boy for the first time, the smile on Noah's face as the infant had felt and heard his own stomach growl, Jonah counting the number of chubby leg rolls and squeezing each one of them to make his son laugh. There'd been so many of those moments and not enough at the same time. He never should've accepted the assignment to Afghanistan. Maybe if he hadn't—if he'd stayed—Noah would still be here. But now the hardened deputy district attorney in front of Jonah was asking him if he'd put his own life in danger for their child or for her, and he couldn't ignore the hint of past vulnerability breaking the evenness of her voice. "I didn't want to lose either of you."

Not again.

THE SUPERFICIAL CUT across her head stung as Madison ran a brush through her wet hair. White marble gleamed across the two-sink vanity stocked with fresh towels, fragranced lotions and a single bottle of cinnamon-spiced aftershave. Turquoise tile surrounded the spacious walk-in shower and the wall behind the freestanding tub, white hexagon tiles heating under her feet. This bathroom—this cabin—had been built and decorated with every luxury she could imagine. From the massive wall of windows in the master bedroom right down to the color of the wood running the length of the entire structure. There was an atmosphere of comfort here, so thick she could see herself on solid ground. Steam clung to the wood-framed mirror over the sink she'd chosen to use to put herself back together. Only she wasn't sure that was possible this time.

Small scratches stood bright against the backdrop of the deeper olive tones of her skin, down her neck, across the backs of her hands. She could still feel the heat of the blast that'd singed across her arms. Parting the luxurious robe she'd found hanging from a hook beside the shower, too big for her, Madison curved her palms over the protruding bump of her belly. Not a scratch. Not a bruise. How much worse would her injuries have been if Jonah hadn't been there? Would she have been able to get herself out of the courtroom if another marshal had taken the judicial security assignment this morning? The answer was already on the tip of her tongue as she recalled his expression when she'd asked if he'd risked his life for her or for their baby. It'd been as though he'd taken the weight of the entire world on at that moment and could barely keep himself upright. Seeing the reserved, practical marshal who'd saved her life—who'd been her friend for so long—break in front of her had crumbled the defensive strategy she'd prepared for herself faster than the attack had. Right then, the walls she'd built to keep herself and this baby safe from dependency had cracked, and she wasn't sure, when it came to Jonah, she'd ever be strong enough to repair them.

Madison hugged the oversize robe around her tighter, hints of that cinnamon-spiced aftershave tickling the back of her throat, and stepped back into the master bedroom. The cathedral ceiling stretched overhead as she paved a trail across the pure white comforter and sheets expertly tucked over the king-size bed with her fingers. She didn't know what it was about this room in particular, how she was supposed to feel being here. She and Jonah weren't together. They weren't lovers. They weren't friends. Why would he bring her here? The United States Marshal Service had safe houses all over the state. He could've taken her to any number of them, but he'd brought her to a place that obviously meant more to him than he'd let on before. Was this where he intended to raise their baby if she'd agreed to him being part of her life?

Dressing in an oversize pair of sweatpants and a T-shirt she'd found in the massive walk-in closet, Madison skimmed the rich gray carpet with her bare toes. Aches and pains stiffened her steps as she circled the large master bedroom. It was perfect in every way. Spacious, welcoming, warm with the fireplace in the corner. The white trim and gray walls soothed the nervous energy skittering up her spine and urged her to fall back on the bed to rest. To stop the constant analysis of each and every moment she and Jonah were together, stop trying to read between the lines and questioning his motives, stop fighting and just…be. When was the last time she'd let herself be still?

The entire cabin was a representation of everything she'd imagined as a child, but reality had never allowed for such dreams. Survival won out over fantasy every day her mother allowed herself and her only daughter to take the abuse her father had handed out. As if they'd deserved the pain for merely existing.

But Madison wasn't that scared little girl anymore.

She'd taken scholarships to put herself through law school, worked harder than any other classmate to get herself on the path to district attorney and vowed never to let anyone get in her way or hold her back. The truth was she couldn't stop. Not until she proved herself. To her father, who'd promised she'd always be useless, helpless and have to rely on him to get through life, to anyone who'd looked her in the face and told her she'd never have the determination, talent or drive to follow through with her dreams. That they were impossible for a woman like her. One mistake. That was all it'd take, and her future would be ripped out from under her.

It wasn't this room asking for her to give in. It was the man who'd brought her here, the marshal she'd put aside everything she believed in for the smallest chance of experiencing what it would feel like to be cared for.

Madison wrenched the bedroom door open harder than she intended and ran straight into a mountain of muscle on the other side. Warmth shot through her as she clasped onto his arm to stabilize herself. Jonah. Strong muscle flexed under her hand, and her mouth dried as memories of how those muscles surrounded her six short months ago lit up in her brain. She stepped back. "I didn't realize you were outside the door."

"I wasn't spying on you if that's what you're worried about," he said.

She hadn't thought of that. "Well, I wasn't until now."

"I wanted to bring you something to eat. I'm not sure if anything makes you nauseous or sick right now, so I tried to stick to some basics I had in the fridge. I got you some strawberries, cashews and crackers." His deep, rumbling laugh invaded the cracks in the wall she'd had to hide behind each time she'd run into him in the courthouse. Jonah stared down at the plate in his hand. "I didn't have any of those chips you like, but I had some dill pickles in the fridge. Thought you might like those, as well."

He'd done all this for her? She reached for the plate, that same heat coiling in her belly charging up her neck and into her face. She couldn't think of a single instance where someone had made her a full-blown meal, not even as a child. She'd mostly lived off of whatever'd she been able to barter from her school friends. Clutching the plate to her middle with both hands, as though she could use the glass as a shield against him, she leveled her chin parallel with the floor. "Thank you. For everything. Not just the food."

"It's the least I can do seeing as how you're one of the few people who can have me fired." He leaned against the door frame with that gut-wrenching smile she couldn't get enough of in place. The way he was looking at her right then… It almost felt as though the past few months hadn't happened, that nothing had changed between them, and a comforting familiarity washed through her. She'd missed that, but more than that, she'd missed him. That smile of his, the way he always seemed to be trying to read her mind. The slide of his hand against her arm when he'd tried to stop her from going ahead of him while he was assigned to escort her out of the courthouse. At first, she'd withdrawn into herself and battled to keep her distance, but after a while, she'd come to crave that touch, that connection to him.

Then she'd found out she was pregnant.

Madison carved a dent into her index finger with the edge of the plate he'd handed her. "Have the police been able to trace the caller who took credit for the bombing?"

"Call came from a burner phone purchased about thirty minutes prior to the bombing from one of the electronics stores around the block. Paid in cash. No security footage and the phone has been turned off," he said.

"It's untraceable." She'd prosecuted enough cases to know the phone would be a dead end, but it wasn't nothing. There was a chance—however small—that when the bomb squad analyzed and re-created the device, they'd be able to follow the incoming call to the phone used to detonate the bomb. Perhaps the bomber had made a mistake in using the same phone to trigger the device and make the call to take credit for the devastation. "How many dead?"

An emptiness slipped into his gaze, and her heart jerked in her chest at the rapid change. So different from the swirl of blue she'd gotten used to when he looked at her, but she couldn't blame him either. Lives had been taken right in front of them, the echoes of their screams still clear in her head. "Eight so far. Victims who were sitting closest to the device in the gallery. Some media, a few family members. Twenty-six wounded, one in critical condition."

"Have the marshals been able to find the judge or the bailiff?" Getting a new judge to take on this case would alter the timeline of sentencing the Rip City Bomber for what she'd done. Madison couldn't afford to have the case take another year, and Rosalind Eyler deserved to rot behind bars sooner rather than later.

"Turns out the bailiff saved the judge's life. Got him out of there right before the bomb detonated." Jonah straightened, suddenly so much… bigger than she remembered. "I checked that entire courtroom and the schedule, Maddi. The preliminary hearing time wasn't announced to the public until an hour before court proceedings started. There was no way someone outside of the case could've gotten into that courtroom to plant the device in the HVAC system."

She nodded, still clutching the plate in her hands. It wasn't his words she had to focus on but the meaning, too. Whoever'd triggered that bomb had intimate knowledge of her, her schedule and the case. Only a handful of people were privy to that information, but no one she would've suspected to try to kill her. She couldn't forget the bomber had called to take credit in the Rip City Bomber's name, too. Why? "The HVAC system would've been put in during the courthouse's construction. The crew finished a month ago. Whoever planted the device only would've had access to that location if it'd been open."

"I'll have my team look into the contractors and their employees and anyone who might've toured that courtroom up until it was finished." He reached out, taking her hand between both of his, and her stomach flipped. "In the meantime, we can't discount the possibility Rosalind Eyler has wanted you dead from the beginning and will do whatever it takes to walk free. Either way, I'm not going to let that happen."

Chapter Four

Jonah shoved the tablet away from him across the coffee table. Heat crawled up the back of his neck from the wood-burning stove a few feet behind him. After scrubbing the hollows of his eyes with calloused palms, he set his elbows on his knees.

According to Deputy Marshal Dylan Cove—the newest marshal in the Oregon division—the construction crew who'd been contracted to build the new courthouse had all checked out. Each and every single one of them. As a former private investigator out of the east, Cove had the ability to dig past the surface. He was more than capable of uncovering the truth, but nothing had jumped out at Jonah as he reviewed the deputy's report. Not a single worker on that job site had a connection to the Rip City Bomber as far as Cove had been able to tell. No financial struggles. No blackmail material. Nothing that got Jonah closer to finding who'd targeted Madison and his baby. "Damn it."

"And here I was under the impression only Marshal Reed believed he was a superhero, what with him wearing those shirts all the time." Madison's sweet voice, so clearly tinted with exhaustion, soothed the frustrated energy climbing up his spine. She was supposed to be resting, taking it easy. But one thing he'd learned about Madison Gray over the years was that she didn't know the meaning of slowing down. From the moment her feet hit the floor in the morning to the minute she closed her eyes at night, she'd dedicated her entire career—her life—to serving justice. Same as he had, but their shared professional interest was only one of the things that'd brought them together.

Jonah interlaced his fingers, driving them down the bridge of his nose, then to his chin as he raised his gaze to meet hers on the open second-level landing. "I'd tell you you're supposed to be sleeping, but I've known you long enough to know I'd probably have a high heel thrown at my face if I dared question your work habits."

"This basketball you so elegantly implanted in my uterus makes it hard to sleep anymore." Long fingers curled over the edge of the banister, the sweats and T-shirt she'd picked out from his closet hiding the lean figure underneath. Having pulled her hair back, she accentuated the scrapes and bruises along her cheek, head and neck, and his gut clenched. "His late-night dance parties ensure I have to use the bathroom in thirty-minute intervals."

Jonah's hands dropped between his knees as he stared up at her. Shock held him in place as the past rushed to meet the present. "Did you say 'his'?"

Rolling perfect lips between her teeth, Madison took to the stairs until she stood in front of him. A rush of heat that had nothing to do with the stove behind him exploded from his chest. "I found out a few weeks ago. I didn't want to wait. I'm… We're having a boy."

"We're having a boy." He couldn't believe it, but more important than that, for the first time she'd included him in the pregnancy. She wasn't having a boy. They were. "That's…" He didn't know what to say. Jonah stepped into her, wrapping her in his arms. Rigidity infused the muscles down her back a moment before she relaxed into him, and the world, the investigation, the fact they'd barely walked out of the courthouse alive this morning faded. The sweet scent of peach tickled the back of his throat, instantly throwing him back to that night they'd taken their friendship to the next level, and his gut tightened.

She settled back onto the four corners of her toes, her mouth a mere two inches from his. Her exhale tangled with his as time froze, stretching into a comfortable beat from one second to the next. Those mesmerizing caramel eyes flickered up to his, and before he had the chance to close the space between them, she rose up onto her toes and set her mouth against his.

His heart stopped as she slipped her tongue past the seam of his lips and reminded his addictive neural pathways how she tasted, but before he had a chance to process what'd changed in these last few minutes, Madison pulled back.

"I'm sorry. I didn't mean… I don't know what I was thinking." A humorless laugh escaped from between her lips as she seemingly forced her hand to slip from his uninjured shoulder. "This day has been…a lot, and I had no right to try to make myself feel better about what happened by misleading you again."

Again. Right. Because whatever'd happened between them hadn't meant anything, wouldn't ever mean anything, to her. This was another classic example of simply biology. She'd been through hell today and barely survived. Her nervous system was craving something familiar, something soothing, and he had no reason to believe whatever connection they'd had would be anything more than superficial.

"I understand." Jonah stepped back, the feel of her hips still a phantom weight in his palms. Hell. Reality bled into focus. One slip in involving him in this pregnancy didn't change the fact she'd make sure to go out of her way to raise this baby alone. As much as it hurt to know what they'd had together would stay in the past, she'd made it perfectly clear she wasn't willing to make room in her life for him. When this investigation was finished, she and the baby would move on with their lives. Without him. That was what she wanted, and short of meeting her on the other side of a courtroom similar to the one they'd nearly died in this morning, he'd concede to her wishes. "I'm really happy for you, about the baby."

"Thank you." Brushing a stray strand of hair behind her ear, she stepped toward the tablet still glowing from the coffee table and bent to read the screen. "The deputy you asked to look into a viable suspect from the construction crew didn't find anything tangible. No motives, no sudden influx in bank deposits, or connections between the Rip City Bomber and any of them. Nothing more than a few parking tickets and one DUI." She swiped her index finger across the screen to continue through the report. "The chemical composition of the courtroom bomb matches the makeup of the Rip City Bomber devices. Looks like Marshal Cove's leading theory is Rosaline Eyler is trying to sway the jury in her favor. Prove whoever set off those four bombs around the city is still out there while she's behind bars."

Jonah forced himself back into the headspace to work this case and cleared his throat. "You're the one prosecuting the case, Counselor. You've seen the evidence. Investigators logged four empty beakers with ammonium nitrate residue from Rosalind's laboratory into evidence after the Portland Police Bureau connected four victims from the bombings back to the pharmaceutical company they worked for. She's a former chemist who ensured anyone who'd used her research to get promoted above her didn't make it out of the explosions alive. Along with twenty-eight other innocent victims. Rosalind Eyler is intelligent, determined and doesn't care how many people she has to hurt to get what she wants, but she made a mistake. She got caught. It's not hard to imagine her work didn't end with that fourth explosion. She wants to finish what she started, and she'll do whatever it takes ensure she can."

"Makes sense." Seconds passed. Maybe a minute before Madison moved. "You know, I've prosecuted over one hundred and fifty cases for the DA's office. I've put away murderers, abusers and drug dealers and made sure every single one of them answered for what they've done."

Crackling fire from the stove highlighted and shadowed the angles of her features as she read the rest of the report. Vulnerability swirled in her gaze as she turned toward him, something he'd never witnessed from the deputy district attorney before. Tears glittered with help from the flames in the stove, and his fingers automatically flexed into fists. Ready to confront whatever nightmares had put them there for her. "Every day I walk out of those courthouse doors, I can't help but wonder if I did enough to make a difference. I wonder if there'd been a prosecutor driven and strategic enough, someone who could see the threat my father posed to his own wife and daughter, that things would've been different. That instead of being afraid for her own life, my mother would've been happy, that she would've had the ability to see that I was right there waiting for her to choose to be with me instead of crawling back to him over and over again. I wanted someone to fight for me. Just once."

Jonah had tried fighting for her—for them—and she'd pushed him away. Didn't she see that?

"I don't care who's behind this." The vulnerability vanished, the prosecutor he'd come to admire in the courtroom taking her place. "I'm not going to let them stop me for being here for my son or for being the prosecutor the next little girl in my situation needs." She took the seat he'd vacated a few minutes ago and pulled the tablet into her lap. "The construction crew might not have any connections to the Rip City Bomber on the surface, but that doesn't mean someone else who had access to that courtroom won't."

This, right here, the late nights, the careful poring over of case files, the orders-in from restaurants around the courthouse… This was Madison in her element. Didn't matter how tired she'd get, how long she'd gone without eating, how many times he'd tried to convince her to take a break, she wouldn't quit until she was positive about the next step she had to take in the case. All those assignments to escort her from the courthouse had started out exactly like this. Dark, quiet, just the two of them. She'd always have a homemade crossword puzzle waiting for him to solve to keep him from getting bored while she worked, but what she failed to realize was that he'd been the one to ask for as many judicial security assignments as he could get. Until one night as he'd walked her to her vehicle, she'd hesitated getting in, turned to face him and pulled him in for a kiss he'd never seen coming. She'd changed everything.

Madison pulled the coffee table closer, never taking her eyes off the tablet screen. It was going to be a long night, and there wasn't anything he could do or say to slow her down. Jonah headed toward the kitchen. "I'll get today's crossword from the paper."

A POP FROM the wood-burning stove ripped her from unconsciousness.

Madison blinked against the onslaught of incoming sunlight through the floor-to-ceiling windows in the main living space. Closing one eye in an automatic attempt to dim the sudden blindness, she searched the living room where she and Jonah had spent a good portion of the night narrowing down a list of suspects motivated to trigger that device in the courtroom. The one she almost hadn't survived. The couch where she last remembered him sitting was empty, a blanket thrown off to one side.

He'd stayed up with her through the night. Just like he had countless times when he'd been assigned to escort her out of the courthouse the past few years. Before she'd ruined everything.

Pushing upright in the chair, she stretched her neck to one side. A power cord now ran from the tablet she'd been working on that had died a few hours into her deep dive into the case. Lucky for her, she'd practically memorized everything she needed to know about the Rip City Bomber investigation and had been able to switch over to pen and paper to keep running through all the new angles. Except there was a possibility whoever'd set that bomb in the courtroom was merely hiding behind Rosalind Eyler's name and not connected to the former chemist at all. At least not directly. Or Rosalind had lied about not having an accomplice to help her get her revenge.

No. There had to be something more going on here. The Rip City Bomber's attacks had followed a pattern. One explosion every month until Rosalind had been caught, and this one didn't fit.

Too many suspects. Not enough motive for any of them, but she and Jonah had been able to narrow down the list considerably by eliminating financial backers of the company hired for the new construction of the courthouse. That still left the possibility the Rip City Bomber herself had been involved, however far-fetched considering Rosalind Eyler had been arrested six months ago. Madison couldn't discount a copycat, a partner or a grieving family member who felt they didn't have any other option to find justice, but a motive for wanting her dead had yet to jump out at them.

"Oh, good. You're up." That voice. His voice. It slid through her, reaching into all the dark corners she'd cut herself off from years ago, and lit up her insides. He set a steaming mug of slightly browned tea on the coffee table, the scent familiar and comforting. Greek tea with lemon and honey. Her favorite. But there was no reason he'd have it here, and this tea wasn't on grocery shelves. "I was worried my online order of dill pickle chips wouldn't get here before you came out of your coma."

"I was snoring, wasn't I?" Running one hand back through her hair, she reached for the mug. Heat tunneled deep into her hands and up her arms, but the embarrassment of knowing she'd once again fallen into a situation where he'd had to suffer through her relentless snoring rose into her neck and face.

"Not too bad." His rich, deep laugh swirled through her as he took his seat on the couch across from her. With his own mug in hand, he looked every bit the man she'd gotten to know after she'd woken up beside him in bed one morning. Quick to smile, playful at times and sexy as hell. So different from the marshal he put on for the world. "Enough for me to remember to add earplugs to my order before I hit Submit."

"I'm sorry. It's worse now with the baby. He's always trying to find ways to evacuate my lungs for more space." A smile tugged at the corner of her mouth, and Madison physically felt the atmosphere change between them. Just as it had that night she'd taken him back to her house. With one lapse in judgment, she'd suffocated what she'd considered her only real friendship and turned it into something neither of them had been prepared for. She adjusted to accommodate the pins and needles climbing up the foot under her opposite thigh and took a sip of her tea. Perfect amount of honey and lemon to bring her back into the real world.

She shouldn't have kissed him last night. She'd just…needed to forget the memories of fire and debris and blood. If only for a few seconds. But she hadn't worked to get away from her father's control only to be trapped by another man, this one with a gut-wrenching smile and a claim to the life growing inside her. No matter how much a deep part of her battled to let her defenses down, to remember what it'd felt like to be the center of Jonah's entire world that night, she couldn't make that mistake again. Her future counted on it.

"I'm used to working through the night, but I'll make sure to keep the snoring behind closed doors as long as we're stuck here together." She stood, mug in hand, as she maneuvered her way back toward the kitchen. "Does one of these massive rooms have a desk I can take over? Might be easier for you to get some sleep if I quarantine myself somewhere upstairs."

Setting her nearly full mug on the cool granite of the kitchen island, she forced herself to breathe evenly as awareness spiked her blood pressure higher. She didn't have to turn around, didn't have to face him to know he'd followed her during her retreat.

"Maddi, we've already tried that, remember? For five months," he said. "But you know as well as I do that no amount of hiding is going to solve anything between us."

She did know that. Because no matter how many times she'd dodged having to speak to him in the courthouse, no matter how many times she'd declined his calls, this tension between them wasn't going to fix itself. She wasn't sure what would, but she didn't have the energy to confront the truth now. "Is that because you'll still be able to hear me snoring through the door?"

Warm hands framed her hips, and it took everything she had left not to lean back, to give in, to…have him take care of her for a little while.

She stared at the cup of tea he'd made her, determined to hold her ground. To prove she could. To prove he didn't have this invisible, illogical grip on her she'd never be able to escape. His breath wisped across the oversensitized skin of her neck and face. "You snore as loud as a chain saw, but you're not a bear in heat."

Laughter burst from her chest, and the hollow, controlled, perfectionistic piece of herself she'd used to drive herself into the DA's office threatened to break. This was how it'd always been between them. Him on one side of a blade, her on the other. Their professional interests had brought them into each other's perfectly balanced ecosystem, but too much one way and she'd tip. She'd lose herself and everything she believed in. He was right before. He wasn't her father, and there hadn't ever been a single moment when she'd feared for her safety—not physically—with Jonah, but the thought of relying on someone else, of depending on them not to hurt her when she'd been wrong so many times before, was too much. Her smile faded as she put her shields back in place. Madison turned in his hands, faced him as she'd face any defendant in the courtroom, and stared up at him. "Tell me why you want to co-parent this baby with me, Jonah. Why do you keep pushing me to see things your way? Why is it important to you? And keep in mind 'because that's the way it's supposed to be' isn't an argument you can win."

A sudden coolness swept across his expression. Not stoic or guarded as she'd expected but something deeper, something that almost…stunned her. His palms fell away from her hips, and he took one step back in retreat. In her next breath, he offered her his hand. "Let me show you."

"Okay." Four simple words, but she couldn't decipher the meaning behind them. Slipping her hand into his, she let him lead her around the base of the massive grand staircase and up to the second level. Light-colored wood branched off toward each of the bedrooms as Jonah tugged her into the wing of the cabin she hadn't gotten a chance to explore for herself. Two bedrooms were positioned on this side of the house.

He headed straight for the only door that'd been closed. Hesitation tensed the muscles across his shoulders and pulled the fresh gauze she'd patched over his wound above the collar of his shirt. "We've known each other a long time, but no one, not even the other marshals in my district, know about this."

Light speared into the hallway as he pushed the door wide and waited for her to step inside. Dust floated like falling snowflakes as she rounded the door frame, so distracting from the rest of the space. Every inch of the room had been meticulously designed. From the white dresser and curtains, to the artwork positioned above a crib on the largest wall. A glider in deep-colored fabric pulled at her attention as she struggled to control her breathing.

A nursery.

"I don't... I don't understand. What is this?" This didn't make sense. Her fingers curled into fists as she took in the smallest details and tried to counter the sudden image of her sitting in that damn glider with their son. Heat flared across her skin as she turned on him. "You built a nursery for our baby knowing I wanted to raise him on my own. This is why you've been pushing me to give in to what you want? Because you already put together a place for him to sleep?"

Had this been the reason he'd brought her here after the attack? All this time, she'd believed he had been giving her space, that he respected her decision, but that wasn't it at all. He'd been waiting for the moment to reveal what he wanted when it came to raising their child. How could she have been so stupid? They'd been friends for years, but she'd never truly known the man standing in front of her. "If you think you can win a custody battle with me in court, you have no idea—"

"I didn't put this nursery together for our son, Maddi." His voice hollowed as he stared out over the top of her head, and her stomach twisted. "I built it for my first son a few years ago. Right before he died."

Chapter Five

He hadn't told anyone. Hadn't revealed it to the FBI when it'd happened. He'd simply packed up his belongings in the small room he'd taken over at Shindand Air Base seventy-five miles from the Iranian border and gotten on a plane to come home. But he'd been too late. He forced himself back into the moment, back from the anger, the desperation, the loss clawing him to shreds inside. Back into this room he hadn't stepped inside since he'd buried his son. It'd been easy to fall into the comforting black hole of numbness he'd found over the years, to pretend he'd moved on and grieved. Until he'd met Madison.

Color drained from her face, her mouth parted. "You never told me you had a son."

"I don't." The finality of that statement hit him as hard as a punch to the gut and left him just as breathless. Jonah studied the gold animal figures on the dresser he'd spent hours searching for across the city two days before he'd left for Afghanistan. A giraffe. An elephant. This nursery was supposed to be a safe place for Noah. Instead it'd been where he'd died. "Not anymore."

"I'm so sorry, Jonah. I had no idea." Her voice softened, keeping him anchored. Supported. Still dressed in the oversize T-shirt and sweats she'd borrowed from his closet, Madison smoothed her hands over her growing belly and accentuated the roundness of her pregnancy. "Will you tell me what happened?"

"I wasn't here." The last memories he had of his son now were the ones he wanted to forget. The phone call telling him Noah had passed away, the race to the airstrip, the long flight across the ocean. He swiped his hand across his face to keep the grief at bay, to protect himself from feeling that pain again, but the past twenty-four hours had destroyed his defenses. "My entire life I've known I wanted a family. I wanted what my parents had. Not just a marriage but a friendship, someone I could wake up next to every morning and be thankful she was part of my life. Someone I could laugh with and raise children with, but working for the FBI kept me on the road ninety percent of the time. It was hard to meet people in my line of work. Most of the time we're running toward the explosions, not away from them, so that tends to put a damper on long-term relationships. I wasn't ready to give up my career and I'd accepted a life partner probably wouldn't be in the cards for me, but I still felt like there was a part of me missing. So I looked into adoption." He exhaled hard, fighting to gain some kind of control. "Miraculously, a teenage birth mother chose me to adopt her baby. I was there with her when she gave birth. I was the first one to hold him. I got to hear him cry for the first time. He was…everything, and after a couple of days of observation in the hospital, I was able to take him home."

Madison slipped her hand into his and squeezed, eliciting a similar effect in his chest as he swallowed the swelling in his throat. "What was his name?"

"Noah. We had two weeks together before the FBI assigned me to Afghanistan, and I loved every minute of it. I felt like the missing piece I'd been living with my whole life didn't hurt as much." He lowered his gaze to the floor, watching specks of dust dance between them. "As much as I hated the idea of leaving him with my parents for three months, Afghanistan would've been my last assignment for the Bureau. As soon as I got home, I'd planned on putting in my resignation, and Noah and I could live out here full-time." He nodded. "I was five days into my assignment when my mom called me with the news."

Madison's spine straightened a bit more. "How did it happen?"

He remembered every word out of his mother's mouth, every hitch in her breathing over the staticky line, every sob that escaped her chest. She hadn't been able to even say the words until he'd begged her to tell him what was wrong. "He'd passed away in his sleep in the middle of the night. Peacefully, as far as the medical examiner was able to tell, but she couldn't tell me any more than that without doing an autopsy. Sudden infant death syndrome. Something I hadn't known existed until it'd happened to my own son."

"I can't imagine how much pain you've gone through. I'm so sorry." Releasing his hand, Madison closed the distance between them. She rose onto her tiptoes and wrapped her arms around his neck, her pregnant belly grazing his stomach. A soft kick reverberated through him as he held on to her with everything he had, and his heart jerked in his chest. "Why didn't you tell me?"

"SIDS isn't genetic. There was no reason to tell you until you wanted to know." Jonah closed his eyes as their baby kicked at him again. He hadn't ever had the privilege of watching a chosen partner grow the life they'd created together, and he couldn't seem to let go. In less than three months' time, Madison would give birth to their boy, and it was up to her to decide who'd be there for her. "In truth, I didn't know what to say. I wanted you to see I respected your decision to raise this baby on your own without being pressured into doing something because of my past, but now you know, and I'll understand if that doesn't change your plans."

"You haven't pressured me, Jonah." She slid from his arms, staring up at him with vivid empathy in her light brown gaze. "You saved my life, and I will never be able to repay you for that, but my decision hasn't changed. I'm going to support this baby on my own. As much as I want to give you what you want, to give this baby a home with two parents, I can't ignore everything I've overcome to get to this point."

The back of his throat burned. He'd known, even as he'd recounted what'd happened to Noah, that there was a chance Madison wouldn't change her mind. She was the most determined, intelligent, hardworking woman he'd ever met, and to think she'd budge so easily would've been against everything he'd come to admire about her. "I understand."

"But…" Her gaze dropped toward his chest. "After knowing how hard you fought to get Noah, and hearing how short of a time you were able to spend with him before he died, I'm willing to have my lawyer look into drafting a visitation arrangement."

What? "Why would you do that?"

"As much as I've wanted to keep this baby

for myself and have wanted to prove I could do this alone, it took both of us to make him." She smoothed her palms over her stomach, highlighting the small bubble of her belly button being pushed outward by their son. "It was unfair of me to ignore your feelings about our circumstances. He's your son as much as he is mine, and he deserves to know how much his father loves him, even if you aren't living in the same house as we are."

Surprise coursed through him. This was what he'd wanted, what he'd worked so hard for. "Are you sure you can live with that? Seeing me every other weekend, or whatever the arrangement will be, having me in your life?"

"The worst part of growing up in the house that I did with two emotionally immature parents was not knowing if they loved me. I don't ever want our son to have to question if his parents cared about him." She lifted her chin a notch higher to meet his gaze. "My decision had nothing to do with you, Jonah. With all those late nights and long drives to and from the courthouse, you became the only person I've trusted, that I could count on to be there when he said and do what he'd said he'd do. You make me feel safe. Having you there in my office was enough to make me feel anchored, and I'd be lying to myself if I said I didn't want more of that in my life. That night I asked you to come back to my place was everything I'd imagined." A burst of laughter rolled up her throat. "And more, obviously."

He stepped into her, placing his hands on either side of her growing belly, and every cell in his body hummed in satisfaction. Having her here, in this room, with their baby between them. It was… perfect. "Obviously."

"But as soon as I saw the two blue lines on the pregnancy test, I knew that would be the end." Her voice neutralized, an emotional calm sliding into her eyes. "You're not my father. I know that. There isn't a single part of me that believes you'd ever hurt me, but I can't put myself in the position my mother did every time she was forced to crawl back to him. I want you to know your son, Jonah, and I'm willing to give a visitation agreement a try, but I won't let you use our son to force something more between you and me."

"What is that supposed to mean?" Nausea rolled through him. He didn't understand. "Everything we had before the pregnancy, you want to, what… pretend it never happened? That we were never friends, that all those long hours meant nothing?"

"I have to." She stepped out of his reach, his fingers tingling for the warmth from her elevated body heat. Long sleek hair shifted over her shoulder as she took a deep breath. "I'm sorry. The truth is I've missed you. I've missed our late nights together and spending the early morning hours creating a homemade crossword puzzle for you to keep yourself busy with while I work, but I think we were both better off as colleagues than we were as lovers. And I think that's how our relationship needs to stay going forward, especially if you're going to be visiting our son. I don't want there to be any confusion. For any of us."

He'd known not to expect her to change her mind about fully supporting the baby, but to erase an entire two years' worth of inside jokes, horrible takeout and case comparison in an instant was... too much to take. The numbness he'd relied on to get him through the past few years spread, and Jonah willingly fell into the safe space he'd created. "In that case, Counselor, I should follow up with my team and figure out who the hell is trying to kill you."

Jonah turned toward the bedroom door and strode from the nursery.

COUNSELOR.

A stone sank deep in her stomach as she read through the Rip City Bomber case files on her tablet, Jonah's expression still engraved in her mind. He'd lost a son, a baby she'd had no idea existed, but the cold hardness etched into the finer lines of his face when she'd cut off the possibility of them being more than parents churned queasiness in her stomach.

She couldn't focus on that right now. A bomb had detonated in the courtroom where she'd been prosecuting the biggest case of her career, and she'd gotten no closer to narrowing the suspect pool than she was a few hours ago. She'd run through Rosalind Eyler's connections, acquaintances, every suspect she could possibly think of—twice—and had come up empty. If the Rip City Bomber had set the device herself, how would Rosalind have done it? How would she have pulled those strings from behind bars? The words on the screen blurred in Madison's vision. She set the tablet on the king-size bed she'd spread her paperwork out on after her conversation with Jonah, hints of that cinnamon spice wafting in the air.

Having the marshal assigned to protect her—the father of her baby—this close had warped her sense of self-preservation the past twenty-four hours. Every touch, every inch closer, had hiked her physical awareness of him into overdrive until all she'd felt was him. Not the deputy US marshal who'd been assigned to clear that courtroom. Not the special agent trained to analyze and re-create IEDs in Afghanistan for the FBI. But Jonah. The man who'd treated her with such care the night they'd conceived their son, the one who'd laughed at her horrible jokes, who'd gone out of his way to make her the perfect cup of tea downstairs after a long night of reviewing the case. The man who'd trusted her above all else with the knowledge he'd lost his son after a mere two weeks of parenthood.

She wouldn't apologize for making her needs for complete autonomy when it came to supporting their child clear, but if she was going to get any closer to uncovering who'd targeted her with that bomb, she needed his help. Sliding from the bed, Madison crossed the massive bedroom and descended down the grand staircase into the living room, her heart in her throat.

Movement registered from the kitchen table where he'd set up multiple files and notepads. Muscle corded across Jonah's shoulders through his T-shirt as he put pen to paper, and her insides threatened to melt as phantom sensation surfaced in her fingertips. "The bomb squad has been able to recover and re-create most of the device from the blast. They're still pulling evidence from the rubble and, in some cases, the victims who were closest to the epicenter. If they pull enough together, police might be able pull fingerprints from the individual components."

"You want to be there." She read it in the slight acceleration of his words, the difference in tone from what he'd used with her upstairs, the focus he expended not to face her, and she didn't blame him.

"Protecting you from whoever set that device

and blew up your car is my assignment," he said. "I just do what I'm told."

"And you're regretting pulling me into protective custody after our last conversation." She hadn't meant to say the words, shouldn't have cared about the answer, but there it was. The truth. How could he not knowing he had the expertise to work and possibly solve the bomb investigation but was resigned to staying here with the mother of his child he'd never have a future with? If she were in his position, she wouldn't want to be here either.

"The construction crew and investors backing the contractors were all cleared of motive. There are only two people who benefit having the Rip City Bomber's case thrown out of court, and one of them is the only person allowed access to Rosalind Eyler as long as she's behind bars." Jonah shoved the chair away with the backs of his knees as he stood. "Her lawyer, Harvey Braddock."

Shock replaced the regret that'd brought her downstairs. "You think her defense counsel built and triggered that device during the preliminary hearing?"

"He's a suspect worth looking into, but no one has been able to locate him." Jonah turned ice-blue eyes on her, and the skin of her scalp prickled with the intensity of his focus. "Marshals have surveilled his office, checked the hospitals and morgues, and have been watching his town house downtown. There's been no sign of him since the explosion."

"That doesn't make sense. Rosalind specifically hired Harvey because he's the top criminal defense attorney in the state. He puts in long hours and doesn't stop until he wins or the court makes him stop. He wouldn't up and leave without at least getting another associate to replace him." Madison rolled her lips between her teeth and bit down, a habit she regressed to when she lost herself inside a case. "Besides, killing me with a bomb doesn't automatically get the case thrown out of court, and the caller who took credit for the bombing did so in the Rip City Bomber's name. They wanted us to believe she's behind it. Not convince the jury she was innocent. Harvey wouldn't have wanted any more evidence stacked against his client than he was already up against."

"The only way we're going to make sure is if we find him. You've gone toe-to-toe with Harvey over the years in court," Jonah said. "Any idea where he'd go if he was trying to lie low?"

"We're not friends. Most of the time we only speak when we're in the middle of arguing a case against each other." Snippets of conversation bled into her mind as she tried to recount the discussions between her and opposing counsel from over the course of her career. She lifted her gaze to Jonah, immediately aware of his proximity, and folded her arms across her chest to counter the sudden need to step into him. "There was one time in the past few weeks Harvey talked about getting out of the city once the Rip City Bomber trial concluded. Couldn't wait to show off the beach house he'd inherited from his grandmother to his girlfriend. I'm not sure about the location, but there's a chance the bombing scared him enough to figure who he's really defending and didn't see any other option but to run."

"Any idea who the girlfriend is?" he asked.

"No. He never mentioned her name. At least, not that I can recall." There had to be another way they could locate Harvey. If for no other reason than to make sure he hadn't been injured in the blast. "Can't you get GPS off of his phone?"

"My team already checked. The phone's off." Jonah shook his head, crossing powerful arms over his chest, and an image of all those muscles surrounding the infant in her belly traitorously wormed into her head. "Either the battery died, or Harvey removed it knowing that was the first step we'd take to locate him."

She didn't answer. As much as she'd preferred to work alone, instant satisfaction coursed through her as the past couple of minutes settled between them. She'd missed having someone to talk her cases through with, someone who'd be bound under the same expectations as she was under the law. Someone on her side.

Silence stretched between them, the muscles across her shoulders releasing one by one as she unfolded her arms. Was this how it would be between them from now on? Him on one side and her on the other once their baby was born? Her chest knotted tighter. She'd agreed to have her lawyer draft a visitation agreement, but doubt clutched her insides the longer they stood there. She'd set the boundaries between them for a reason. Why then was it so hard to hold up her end? "How's your shoulder?"

"Is that what you really want to talk about? You've never been one for small talk or social rituals, Maddi. Don't start now." Ringing pierced through the sound of her pulse pounding behind her ears. Had to be his phone. He'd taken hers back at the scene when he'd whisked her into protective custody. Jonah strode to intercept the incoming call, unfolding his arms as he brushed past her. He answered, putting the phone on speaker. "You've got us both, Chief."

"There's been another bombing," Remington Barton said.

Ice shot through Madison's limbs, her gaze locked on Jonah as he turned toward her. For a split second, she couldn't think, couldn't breathe, and she imagined her expression reflected in his.

Another attack. She battled for a single word to fall from her mouth. "Wh-where?"

"Harvey Braddock's home." The deputy chief spelled out the details quickly, her voice even and efficient, and Madison couldn't help but absorb a bit of that calm herself. "Portland police and the FBI's bomb tech are already on the scene. Looks like Mr. Braddock—or someone who'd been using his garage to assemble the device—made a mistake." One second. Two. "One that killed them."

"Harvey?" Madison couldn't believe it. Not after she and Jonah had just walked through all the reasons Rosalind Eyler's attorney should've been innocent. He had no motive other than to introduce reasonable doubt into the case, and taking credit for the courthouse bombing in the Rip City Bomber's name ensured that wouldn't happen. There was something she wasn't seeing yet, a key piece to the puzzle that'd been left out. She closed the space between her and the phone, her arm brushing against Jonah's, and his hand visibly locked around the edges of the phone. "Are you sure it's him?"

"The resulting fire is making it impossible for us to confirm. We don't have all the details or a motive yet, but there's no mistaking someone was building a bomb in the detached garage behind Mr. Braddock's home when the device went off. It's possible he caught someone in the act of trying to set him up, or he'd known the case against Rosalind Eyler wasn't going to end in his client's favor and he'd taken to upping his chances of a win. That'll be up to the FBI to find out." Chief Deputy Barton sighed. "Either way, Harvey Braddock just became the FBI's number one suspect for the bombing at the courthouse, but the bomb squad is short on manpower. The fire department is trying to control the blaze, but it looks like the composition of this device burns hotter and faster than the last one. Only they're not sure with what. The FBI is asking for you, Jonah. You're the one in the state who has the most experience with IEDs."

His eyes shifted to hers, her heart in her throat as the logical part of her brain ran through the angles of what that meant. "I'm not leaving Madison without protection."

"I don't have anyone else who can take over her detail," Remi said. "Not with two bombings in less than forty-eight hours and a manhunt beginning for Harvey Braddock."

Jonah raised the end of the phone closer to his mouth. "Then she's coming with me."

Chapter Six

He caught sight of the flames a block from the scene. There was no way he'd be able to get close to that garage until the fire department could control the blaze, which only left Madison out in the open longer. Not a risk he wanted to take, but Remi had been right. He was the only bomb tech within a few hundred miles who'd had experience with this kind of bomb, and he couldn't ignore the call.

"I've never seen anything like it." Madison stared out the windshield as thick black smoke hit the SUV. Police waved him through the perimeter they'd created at the end of the street, civilians lining the other side of the caution tape. "What kind of chemicals burn so hot it's impossible to put them out with water?"

There weren't many compounds that were that incendiary, but, judging on the slightly acidic burn in the back of his throat and the spread of the flames as they neared the target scene, he'd narrowed it down to one. Jonah pulled to the curb, threw the SUV in Park and pinpointed the garage where firefighters battled the flames spreading up the main house and consuming the neighbor's yard. Bright orange embers smoldered in patches over the driveway. Damn it. "Thermite. Nearly impossible to extinguish, even under water. It can burn through pavement and melt engine blocks, but it doesn't really have the capacity to create a blast radius as large as that one. Whoever built the device must've added another explosive charge to increase the diameter. It'll be hours before they can get those flames under control."

Hours they didn't have.

"How would someone have gotten their hands on enough thermite to create...all this without suspicion? And how would Harvey not have known it was going on in his backyard?" Eyes wide, Madison surveyed the scene with astonishment in her voice. "I thought there were restrictions on the public being able to get even the smallest amounts."

"Harvey would've known, which means he might be the bomber we're looking for after all." Jonah shouldered out of the vehicle, locking his jaw against the pain shooting through his wound, and rounded toward the cargo space. He hefted the hatch overhead and grabbed for the toolkit left over from his days in the FBI. Screwdrivers, drill bits, flashlights and body protection. He wasn't a bomb tech anymore, but muscle memory had already taken control.

The passenger side door slammed closed, and before he had a chance to tell Madison to stay in the SUV, she was at his side. Every five-foot-four stubborn, perfectionistic and beautiful inch of her. "The device in the courthouse didn't have thermite in it."

"Our bomber is testing explosive charges." He hauled his Kevlar over his head, a groan escaping up his throat from the piercing fire in his shoulder. He dropped the weight fast and clamped onto his shoulder with a hard exhale. There hadn't been enough time for the EMTs to assess the shrapnel wound at the courthouse, but sooner or later, he'd have to have Deputy Finnick Reed, a former combat medic, take a look at the damage. "Damn it."

Warmth pierced through his shirt as Madison rested her fingers on either side of his arm to take a look at the wound. "You've bled through the gauze. You should've gotten stitches, but you had to be your insanely responsible self and whisk me off to safety instead."

He laughed. "I take it you wanted me to risk you and the baby while I sat in the back of an ambulance to take care of a minor wound."

"Your Kevlar doesn't think it's minor. Here." She took the brunt of the load from his vest and helped him maneuver it over his head. Trailing a path down his chest with one hand as he strapped the vest into place, she stepped back. "Guess there's no point in asking you not to go in there, am I right?"

"Careful, Counselor. It almost sounds like you might actually care about what happens to me." He unholstered his sidearm, released the magazine and checked the rounds to counter the sudden need to assure her he'd done this dozens of times and survived. "The FBI asked for me because they know I'm the best at this kind of work. If we're going to find out who tried to kill you at the courthouse, I have to know what we're dealing with, and right now, that looks a hell of a lot like desperation. Which is the worst kind of bomber there is. There are no patterns, no rules they're trying to follow, and they escalate quickly. That means more destruction and more innocent lives at risk."

"Desperation?" Her mouth parted. "Who'd be desperate enough—"

"Watson, the chief and the feds are waiting for you to walk them through this particular device's composition while the firefighters try to get this damn thing under control." Deputy US Marshal Dylan Cove hiked his thumb over his shoulder as he pulled up a few feet short of Jonah and Madison. Dark hair and a beard, the color of natural oil, accentuated the haunted gleam of the former private investigator's eyes. Ropes of muscle struggled to tear in two the thin gray shirt he wore under his cargo jacket. As the newest member of the Oregon marshals division, Cove mostly kept to himself, but the past had been clearly etched in his body language and guarded expression. Older than any of the other deputies in the office, the man obviously had some inner demons he still needed to work out, but he made a hell of a marshal. When it came to personal relationships, on the other hand, it seemed only Remington Barton had the power to calm that storm. "Remi wants your prosecutor friend here to stay away from the target scene." Cove's dark gaze cut to Madison. "I can watch her."

"I told the chief Madison stays with me, and I meant it," he said.

"Jonah, it's okay." Her hands were on him again, pulling him back to her side rather than letting him hold his position between her and Cove, and his heart rate dipped back into normal levels. "You might be comfortable running toward the explosions, but I'm not. I'll stay in the SUV, and I'll be here when you get back. I'm sure Deputy Cove is more than capable of keeping me safe."

"Fine." Acceptance ran through him. As much as he didn't like the thought of leaving her safety in the hands of another marshal, putting Madison in proximity to an ongoing burn site wasn't ideal either. He stepped into Cove and lowered his voice.

"There are dill pickle chips in the back seat if she has any cravings, and fruit and water in the cooler. She's my witness, and if anything happens to her while I'm working this scene, I'm going to hold you personally accountable."

Dylan Cove smiled, then slapped Jonah's uninjured shoulder before bringing him in a few more inches. "You're going to want to check that concern of yours, Watson. Your personal feelings for your witness are showing." Two more pats on his shoulder and Cove maneuvered around him. The former private investigator rubbed his palms together as he approached Madison, then stretched one hand to lead her back to the vehicle. "Let's see what kind of snacks Deputy Watson packed for you, Miss Gray."

Madison's gaze stayed on Jonah for a few feet before she climbed back into the passenger side of the SUV. Deputy Cove would protect her, Jonah had no doubt. Because if he didn't, Jonah would make sure the newest marshal to their division never worked another assignment in his career.

Shouts and the constant hiss of the fire hoses pulled him back into the moment. Firefighters had made some progress near the front of the house, but the area around the detached garage where the explosion had originated would be another battle altogether. He caught the attention of his chief deputy and who he assumed would be the special agent in charge on the Bureau side of the investigation. Now that three explosives had been detonated within the Portland city limits, the FBI would want all hands on deck to make sure there wasn't a fourth. Jonah nodded toward Remi as she waved him over and inserted himself into the tight group of investigators. "What do we know so far?"

"Jonah, this is Special Agent Collin Jackson," Remi said.

Jonah shook hands with the agent. "You're the one who convinced the chief to call me in."

"You're a legend back at Quantico," Special Agent Jackson said. "Lucky for us, you've got the experience to deal with this kind of explosive. My team won't be here until morning."

"We haven't been able to get close enough to the garage to collect evidence, but firefighters are making progress. Their only concern right now is to keep the thermite fires from spreading." Remi hooked her thumbs into the shoulder straps of her Kevlar. "Both USMS and the FBI are getting ready to go through the house. We've got confirmation the property belongs to Harvey Braddock, but we can't know for sure the body we spotted inside the garage is him until the medical examiner can get us the ID. There were no other vehicles at the house when we arrived, but that doesn't mean someone else wasn't here before we rolled up. The composition of the two bombs from yesterday and this one are obviously different, but it's too much of a coincidence to believe this explosion and the one at the courthouse aren't linked."

Jonah agreed. There was only one problem. "I initially pegged Harvey Braddock as someone we needed to look into, but his background doesn't show any experience with explosives. No military record or mining. No family members with access to high-burn explosives either, and to create this kind of improvised explosive device, he'd have to have years of training in hazardous materials."

"You're thinking maybe the defense attorney had a partner and that partner killed him, then set off the device to destroy the evidence?" the special agent in charge asked.

"If that's his body in there, sure, or Harvey Braddock wasn't part of the plan at all. He could've discovered or overheard Rosalind Eyler's plans for Madison Gray, and his client instructed her own partner to tie up loose ends, even at the cost of losing her defense counsel." His gut was still telling him the Rip City Bomber was behind this. If they could construct a paper trail back to the source, they'd have proof Rosalind Eyler's attorney—and the Rip City Bomber herself—had targeted Madison at the courthouse. "Any luck on tracing the thermite?"

"One hundred pounds of thermite was stolen sometime last night from a machinery warehouse in northwest Portland." Remi studied the teams trying to put out the fires around the garage. "The shift supervisor called police as soon as he discovered it missing, but most of the Portland Police Bureau officers have been diverted to the scene at the courthouse. We didn't have any reason to break up our manpower for a B&E after what happened downtown."

Jonah studied the pattern of the burns. "We do now."

"What do you mean?" Agent Jackson asked.

"You said one hundred pounds of thermite was stolen." He scrubbed his hand down his face, the heat prickling the exposed skin of his neck. Thermite burned at a temperature around two thousand degrees and destroyed anything and everything in its path. "Whoever triggered the bomb here had to add an additional explosive charge inside the device they'd built to increase the blast zone, leaving less room for the thermite in the container. From what I've seen of this scene and the amount of thermite they're trying to extinguish, the bomber didn't use more than a quarter of what he had on hand."

The deputy chief cut her attention to him. "You're saying—"

"There's a chance this isn't the only device he built," Jonah said.

MADISON TOOK ANOTHER SIP of her water, the heat from the fire burying under the thick collar of her coat and long-sleeved shirt despite the spring breeze filtering through the open door.

Controlled chaos buzzed around her and the marshal Jonah had been reluctant to let watch her. With the passenger side door partly open, she pulled her tablet from her bag and scanned through the files Jonah had forwarded to her one by one. Rosalind Eyler's known associates and family connections, visitor logs from the prison, including those with her attorney's signature, evidence logs from the Rip City Bomber's home, the FBI's extensive profile and interviews with the defendant. She'd been through them more times than she could count. There was nothing here to suggest Rosalind Eyler had kept in touch with a partner or protégé, at least not officially, but the sudden change in MO said this wasn't the work of the Rip City Bomber. Not directly.

Madison raised her gaze to the fire battling for new life every time firefighters thought they'd gotten the blaze under control. Harvey Braddock might've been one hell of a snake in court, but her gut said he couldn't do this. The only thing she'd known him to want more than money was winning cases. Taking credit for the courthouse bombing in the Rip City Bomber's name ensured he'd lose the biggest case of his career.

No. Madison watched the scene through the windshield. Someone wanted her to believe Rosalind Eyler was behind the bombing that'd nearly taken her life and destroyed her car. This one, too. She wasn't sure how Harvey fit into the equation, but having the attorney at both scenes couldn't be a coincidence. Unless… Unless the real bomber was trying to frame the Rip City Bomber for the attack at the courthouse and was using Harvey's garage to push the evidence to reflect that narrative. Harvey could've figured out who'd been trying to set up his client for attempted murder of a deputy district attorney, and the defense counsel had confronted the bomber. Only he'd realized he'd gotten in over his head too late, but that didn't account for the change in composition between the two bombs. None of the devices built by Rosalind Eyler included thermite. Then again… Maybe that was the point.

Firefighters, marshals and local law enforcement rushed between vehicles toward the house, the buzz of the scene transforming into a frenzy. She sat straighter in her seat. Something was happening. EMTs ran toward the fire. Had someone been hurt? Her mind instantly went to Jonah. He was the only technician with enough experience with this kind of explosive. He would've been the first one to suit up and try to get closer to the device. Her stomach dropped. Madison pushed out of the vehicle, her heels wobbling on the uneven pavement. "Deputy Cove, what's going on?"

Marshal Dylan Cove pushed off from the side of the SUV, a water bottle in his hand. Dark eyes narrowed on the frantic upset spreading to the edges of the perimeter. "Good question." He reached for his radio strapped to his vest and compressed the push-to-talk button. "Marshal Cove for Deputy Chief Barton, over."

Static broke through the high-pitched ringing in Madison's ears.

He tried again. "Remington, what the hell is going on in there?"

No answer.

"Try Jonah—Marshal Watson." Pressure built behind her sternum. Jonah had taken point on dozens of IED disposals and detonations. This was what he'd been trained for, and he was damn good at it. He was fine. She had to believe that. Because the only other option was losing the only person who'd made an effort to give a damn about her.

Cove tried the radio again. Nothing but static.

"Something is interrupting the signal. I can't get through." Concern contorted the deputy's expression. Marshal Cove pulled his sidearm from his hip, released the magazine from the weapon and slammed it back into place. "Get in the vehicle and lock the doors. You don't unlock this SUV for anyone other than myself or Deputy Watson—do I make myself clear?"

"Yes." Sweat built at the base of her neck as

she did as instructed, locking herself in the vehicle. Light gray smoke crept along the pavement toward the outer edges of the perimeter where the SUV was parked.

It couldn't have been easy for the bomber to get his hands on this much thermite. Not with so many regulations and restrictions to the public. So whoever detonated this device had to have personal access or they'd stolen it from another source. Madison sat forward in her seat, trying to see through the smoke.

The thermite. Pulling her tablet pencil from her bag, she quickly sketched notes across the digital file on her screen. If the bomber had been at the courthouse scene as Jonah believed, watching to make sure she hadn't made it out of the courtroom alive, they would've known he was with her. With enough research, they could've easily discovered Jonah was the only expert in the field within a hundred-mile radius who'd dealt with thermite in the past, and known exactly how to draw the marshal assigned to protect her out of hiding. With his witness in tow. "It's a setup."

The passenger side window exploded at her right, thick glass cutting across her face and neck as she ducked into the center of the SUV. A scream tore from her mouth. She tried to shield her face with both hands and shoved her tablet between the seat and the middle console. The passenger door swung open. Strong hands ripped her from the vehicle, and she sucked in a lungful of air to scream. A hand clamped over her mouth, forcing her into a wall of muscle. He showed off the detonator in his free hand. "I wouldn't do that if I were you, Ms. Gray. See, your marshal and the rest of his team have just uncovered the second thermite device inside Harvey Braddock's house, and with one press of this button, I have the power to make sure none of them walk out of there alive. You've spent your entire career putting the bad guys behind bars, so I imagine risking innocent lives doesn't sit well with you."

The black ski mask highlighted light green eyes and a narrow face, but anything more than that slipped her attention as bruising pain spread across her face with his grip on her jaw. Quick inhales and exhales hissed through her nose. She tried to shake her head. No. She didn't want that, but the only alternative meant leaving this scene with a man who'd set off three bombs in the past forty-eight hours and killed at least nine civilians.

"Good girl." He leveled his gaze with hers. "Now you're going to do exactly as I say. Nod so I know you understand."

She did.

"Turn around slowly, head toward the back of the vehicle and walk to the end of the block. If you even think about running or signaling one of the officers at the perimeter, the last thing you'll see is that house in flames." He released her. "Go."

Madison turned as he'd instructed and started walking back the way she and Jonah had entered the scene. She kept her gaze down, careful not to make eye contact with any of the remaining Portland Police Bureau officers as they neared the caution tape sectioning off the street from the target scene. Their attention had been diverted to the house, most likely part of the bomber's plan. One wrong move. That was all it'd take, and Jonah would be gone. The fact Harvey Braddock's garage and property were still burning convinced her the man at her back wasn't bluffing. She couldn't let that happen, couldn't risk losing the man who'd pried his way past her defenses with bad jokes and heated kisses.

She'd spent the last five months determined to keep him as far from their son as she could in an effort to satisfy her own insecurities with being able to raise their baby on her own. For what? To prove she didn't need help, to turn herself into a martyr in the name of pride? Jonah hadn't offered to help because he'd been worried their baby would suffer under the care of one parent. Everything he'd done these past two days had shown her he'd only wanted to support her. How hadn't she seen it before now? She'd made a mistake, and now everything they cared about was at risk.

"The black sedan on the right." The trunk popped open as they came into range of the last vehicle parked on the picture-perfect neighborhood street. "Get in."

What? Madison pulled up short. If she got in that trunk, there were no guarantees she'd ever leave. No guarantees she'd make it out alive, that her son would survive. Panic triggered her flight instinct, and she stepped back into her attacker. She twisted into him and shoved at his chest as hard as she could. Her throat swelled. He latched onto her wrists with both hands and forced her closer to the car. "No. No!"

His arms encircled her upper body, and he hefted her feet off the pavement. Another hand cut off her screams as he hauled her feet over the lip of the trunk. Madison kicked out with everything she had, her heel flying into the middle of the road. This had been a quiet neighborhood until a couple of hours ago when a bomb had detonated a few houses down, and now she was being taken in the middle of broad daylight. Someone would hear her. Someone would see what was happening and tell the police. Rough interior fabric burned the backs of her legs as her abductor forced her into the small, dark compartment. She clawed at him, so consumed with the need to get out that she didn't notice the back of his hand swinging toward her face.

Lightning exploded behind her eyes, and she fell back into the trunk. Pain ricocheted through her head and blacked out the edges of her vision. In a swirl of dizziness, she stared up at her attacker, but couldn't judge how far he stood from her. She blinked to clear her head. In vain. He was going to lock her in. He was going to kill her. Madison tried to sit up, but her balance had been compromised. She reached out. "Wait."

"That's going to cost you, Counselor." He slammed the trunk closed, throwing her into darkness.

Chapter Seven

Jonah crouched in front of the device in full bomb squad gear. The weight of the Kevlar and Nomex increased the tension in his wounded shoulder. Every muscle in his body shot into awareness of the fact one wrong move on his part would kill him and bring this entire house down on top of the team at his back. The device was crude, poorly constructed, but, combined with the container of ammonium nitrate, it'd get the bomber's intended destruction done. The remains of the stolen thermite, a deep red-colored powder, had been packed around the secondary explosive inside a large metal can. With another cell phone acting as remote detonator and a battery duct-taped around the outside of the container, all he could do was try to disassemble the pieces before that phone started ringing.

He set the portable X-ray machine on one side of the device and the phosphorus panel to capture the image on the other to get an idea of anything he might've missed from a visual inspection, and stepped back. Whoever'd designed the bomb had placed it in plain sight. They'd wanted law enforcement to find it, and by setting it up inside the house, they ensured a live technician would have to be time on target. That he would have to approach the package in person.

His earpiece crackled from inside the heavy-duty visor, drowning out the soft whirl of the internal fan built into the helmet. He took the photos, then slowly removed the panel and the portable X-ray machine.

The cell phone screen lit up.

Jonah braced for the same ringtone he'd heard seconds before the bomb had been triggered at the courthouse. He couldn't wait to have the X-rays developed to see what they were dealing with. He had to neutralize the threat now.

The thin balaclava under his helmet absorbed the sweat beading in his hairline as he set down the phosphorous panel and X-ray machine and re-approached the device. He couldn't use the bomb squad's pan disrupter as he had on 90 percent of the IEDs he'd come into contact with to set off the device from a safe distance. Not without possibly triggering a thermite burn, and a mineral water bottle packed with C-4 wouldn't extinguish the chemical reaction either. It'd most likely increase the bomb's blast radius.

There was no playbook in the FBI that would tell him how to neutralize a thermite bomb. He'd have to do this one by hand.

He reached for the grouping of wire leading from the back of the phone into the center of the container. He forced himself to breathe evenly, to stay in the moment instead of worrying if Madison and the baby were safe outside in case he made a mistake. Dylan Cove and the rest of the marshals in his division would make sure she kept a safe distance.

His earpiece crackled again. "Watson…problem."

He was running out of time. Any moment that phone could ring and trigger a detonation ten times as destructive as the one from the garage. He traced the brightly colored wiring with the tips of his fingers. "Remi, say that again."

Static filtered through the radio. This secondary device had been positioned in Harvey Braddock's basement. The signal couldn't get through the foundation cement.

Three wires. Three options to disarm the bomb. One mistake, and he'd never hold his and Madison's son. Never have the chance to become the father Noah had deserved in the first place. Red. Green. Yellow. He unpocketed a razor from his toolkit and sliced the duct tape holding the phone to the container apart. Carefully, going slower than he wanted to go, Jonah peeled the phone from the tape.

All three wires popped free.

His heart shot into his throat. Seconds ticked by, a minute. No detonation. Pulse pounding hard behind his ears, he sat back on his heels. Confusion pushed out the logical answer for a split second, but he couldn't ignore the truth staring him in the face. "It's a dummy."

That didn't make sense. Why trigger a very real bomb in the garage, but set up a dummy in the main house with three times the amount of the stolen thermite?

"Watson…now!" Deputy Chief Remington Barton's words sliced through the focused haze he'd developed over countless bomb calls throughout the years. Something was wrong.

The device had never been connected to the power supply, which meant…the bomber had never intended to trigger the device. Realization hit, and he shot to his feet as fast as he could under one hundred pounds of Kevlar and Nomex. Walls with black-and-white photos blurred in his vision as he climbed the stairs from the basement to the main level. Sunlight pulled him toward the open back door, where firefighters were still battling patches of the initial blaze. Two Portland Police Bureau technicians converged on him to help him out of the suit as Remington and Special Agent Collin Jackson jogged to meet him.

He pried the heavy helmet from his shoulders—pain shooting through the wound—and stripped the balaclava from his head. Burnt spring air rushed to cool the sweat building at the base of his neck. He shook his head as he handed off the helmet to one of the other techs. "The device is a dummy. The power supply was never connected. The bomber... He set us up."

"I think you're right." Remi cut her gaze to the special agent at her side. "We believe the thermite was specifically used to lure you to this scene, Jonah. You've worked with this composition before, and the bomber must've known that. He stole the thermite from that warehouse last night in an effort to pull you out of hiding. With your witness."

He froze. Madison. His nerve endings caught fire as he pinpointed his SUV. Empty. He scoured the scene, his heart thrown into overdrive, and noticed Deputy Marshal Dylan Cove. Alone. He shook his head. No. "Where is she?"

"She's missing," Remi said.

A high-pitched ringing filled his ears.

"Jonah." Remi's warning tone barely registered. "It wasn't his fault. He used appropriate response when he couldn't get the rest of the team on the radio."

Jonah stripped out of the rest of his gear as rage

exploded in his chest. He crossed the property faster than he thought possible and pulled his fist back before Cove turned to face him. He socked the deputy with a strong right hook. The former private investigator collapsed to the ground, but before Jonah had a chance to strike again, Remi and Agent Jackson pulled him back. He lunged again. "You were supposed to stay with her! Where is she, Cove? Tell me where she is!"

Cove rolled onto his side, hand massaging his jaw, as Deputies Foster and Reed helped him to his feet. The newest recruit into the Oregon division wrenched out of the other marshals' hold and faced Jonah with nothing but blood on his mouth and a stiff expression in place. "I don't know. The entire scene had gone into overdrive when you'd found the second device inside the house, but the radios were out. I couldn't get a hold of anyone, including you, to find out what was happening. So I made a call. I instructed her to secure herself inside the vehicle and not open the doors for anyone but you and myself. When I returned to the SUV, I noticed the passenger door open and what was left of the window all over the street. She wasn't inside."

Every word out of the marshal's mouth twisted the invisible knife in Jonah's gut deeper. Madison was gone. He closed the space between him and Cove, Remi's grip on his arm tighter than before.

He didn't care what kind of dysfunctional relationship she and Dylan Cove had or what'd happened between them for her to take the marshal's side. He'd spend the rest of his life making sure the deputy never worked a federal case again. "I told you if anything happened to her, I would personally hold you responsible."

Cove held his ground. "I believed you."

"Enough." Remington inserted herself between the two of them. The hard set of the deputy chief's mouth told each of them that was an order, and if any of them took it as anything less, she'd deal with them herself. "We have a very pregnant deputy district attorney missing and a bomber still out there. Blaming each other for what happened won't get us anywhere. Jonah, take Finn with you to search your SUV. There might be evidence in there that will give us an idea who's behind Madison's abduction. Beckett and Cove will gather statements from the officers and civilians outside the perimeter and find out how our suspect managed to slip in and out of this scene without raising suspicion. Stay in radio contact and move quickly. Let's bring her and her baby home as fast as we can."

"It's my baby." Jonah couldn't keep the truth from them any longer. The men and women circled around him had risked their lives for each other over the years. He trusted every single one of them to have his back in the field, only now he needed them to care about Madison as much as they cared about him. He needed them to bring her back. "Madison is pregnant with my baby. She didn't want anyone to know, but I need for you to understand what's at stake for me. I will do whatever it takes to get them back. With or without your help."

"Oh, hell." Beckett Foster, a deputy who'd once carried out fugitive recovery assignment for his own pregnant ex, threaded one hand through his dark hair. The marshal was expecting a daughter in less than a month, and Jonah now understood how insane Beckett had been driven to keep Raleigh and their baby safe from the threat that'd come for them both a few months ago.

The former combat medic and serial killer survivor, Finnick Reed, whistled. "Well, that explains your foul mood over the past few months."

"I'll help you find her, Watson." Dylan Cove stepped into him, then extended his hand toward Jonah in truce. "Even if it's the last thing I do for the marshals service. I give you my word."

Staring down at the deputy's hand, Jonah latched onto the calloused offering and shook. The rage that'd flashed hot and fast fueled a new burst of adrenaline. "Grab your gear."

SHE ROLLED ONTO her left side as the vehicle made a sharp turn. She couldn't tell how long they'd been driving. Minutes. Hours. Time had dissolved to where seconds ran together. Madison groped for something—anything—she could use to pry the trunk lid open, but her abductor had cleaned the space too thoroughly.

Her kidnapper hadn't targeted her randomly. This had been premeditated from the beginning. As soon as she'd walked out of those courthouse doors on her own feet yesterday, she'd acquired a target on her back. She wasn't going anywhere. Not until the bomber decided otherwise. She traced the wiring from the ceiling of the trunk down to the right taillight. Her mother had smuggled her out in the trunks of random vehicles to escape her father enough times in the middle of the night for her to remember the setup of most cars. Manufacturers were mandated to install emergency release tabs more than twenty years ago due to the high number of accidents that occurred with children locking themselves in trunks, but the spot where she expected the release tab to be sliced into her hand. Her abductor had removed the tab.

"Don't panic." Flipping onto her back, Madison closed her eyes and forced herself to breathe in the small space. She wouldn't run out of oxygen here, but she still had to stay focused. The more adrenaline she used, the less energy she'd have to escape once the vehicle stopped. She was going to get out of here. There wasn't any other option. "Think, think, think."

Feeling along the crease where the back seat met the trunk, she slid her fingertips over cold metal. Seat locks. Relief smoothed the jagged edges of panic. She pulled the first one out.

The vehicle's shocks engaged as the car took another unexpected turn onto uneven road. The back seat fell forward, revealing her masked kidnapper behind the wheel. Dirt kicked up alongside the side of the car through the windshield. Not enough to pinpoint where he'd taken her, but she filed the information for later use in case she had to run. She scanned the car's back seat for a weapon and wrapped her fingers around a heavy piece of metal. A crowbar.

Slowly, keeping her eyes glued to the rearview mirror for any sign her captor was aware of what she was doing, Madison pulled the steel across the seat. A metallic hiss as the crowbar caught on the seat's fabric reached her ears but didn't draw the attention of her attacker. Not yet. The car bounced over rough terrain, and she lost her grip on the weapon. It fell forward onto the floor with a deep *thunk*, and light green eyes locked on hers in the mirror.

"Aren't you resourceful?" He slammed on the brakes, throwing her forward, and pushed the vehicle into Park. Shouldering out of the car, her abductor raced around the driver's side toward the trunk.

The moment he hauled that lid open, she'd be out of time. Leveraging her feet against the floor of the trunk, Madison kicked to thrust herself into the back seat. Metal dug into her oversensitive baby bump halfway through as cold air rushed around her ankles. Strong hands wrapped around her calves and struggled to pull her back through the opening. The crowbar. Her heart thundered behind her ears. Stretching one hand down onto the floor, she searched for the weapon blindly while kicking as hard as she could to throw off her attacker. She caught him in the jaw, and he fell back. She dived for the crowbar with one hand and unlocked the passenger side back door with the other. Dragging herself from the vehicle, she stumbled forward. Foreboding knotted tight in her chest. "What…? No."

Trees stretched in each direction. The crush of the nearby falls filled her ears. He'd brought her out into the middle of the wilderness. The sun had already started trailing across the western half of the sky. In a few hours, darkness would consume this entire side of the mountain and temperatures would drop. She wouldn't survive out here on her own. Not before Jonah and his team of marshals had a chance to find her. Madison rolled the crowbar in her hand, twisting as gravel crunched from behind. She didn't have a choice. The woods were her only option.

Sprinting as fast as she could to the trail leading farther up the incline, she held her large pregnant belly with one hand and the crowbar with the other. She'd kept in shape over the last few months, but her workouts had been more weight centered, not sprinting up the side of a mountain, but she pushed herself harder. The iconic Benson Bridge, surrounded by walls of greenery, a white wall of water and rock, overlooked the lower falls and gave her the only chance of cover. She could make it. She had to make it. For her baby. For Jonah to have a chance to be the father that'd been taken from him after Noah had died.

"You're making this more difficult than it needs to be, Madison." Her captor's voice hissed through the trees. "There's nowhere you can run that I won't find you, and when I do, you're going to wish the bomb at the courthouse killed you first."

Cold blasts of wind and spits of water from the falls slapped at her exposed skin. Her fingers numbed from her grip on the crowbar, but she couldn't look back. Snow had started melting weeks ago. The incline was slick with water and mud that suctioned at her bare feet. She was out of breath, running out of energy. Her abductor was more physically fit, not pregnant and closing in fast. She couldn't stick to the trail. She didn't have any skills when it came to hunting, but she understood the basic concept of following a prey's tracks. She was making it too easy for him. Her lungs burned, her throat on fire. She wouldn't make it to the bridge at this pace.

Slipping off the edge of the path, she crept as soundlessly as possible deeper into the wilderness surrounding the falls. Twigs and sharp rocks cut into her feet, but she forced herself to swallow the discomfort. She leaned into a tree slightly thicker than her hips and faced away from the main trail. The crown of her head scratched against rough bark as she clutched the crowbar to her chest.

Footsteps echoed off the rocks around her, and a sob built in her chest. From the last remnants of adrenaline leaving her system or the massive amount of hormones singing through her blood, Madison didn't know. She didn't care. Surviving. That was the only thing that mattered. Her kidnapper was closing in, but she wasn't going to go down without a fight.

Filling her lungs with humid air, she let out her breath as silently as possible before creeping deeper into the woods. She kept the tree she'd used as cover between her and the main trail and slipped off her coat. Instant warning charged through her as she set the heavy material at her feet. Temperatures dropped well below freezing out here in the high wilderness after the sun disappeared beneath the horizon, but the color was too bright compared with the shaded greens and deep browns around her. Without it, there was less chance her attacker would spot her on the run. The sound of her breath strained in her lungs, nearly overtaking the rush of the falls. She stepped back, completely focused on the tree she'd left behind.

A twig snapped under her heel.

Movement registered off to her left a split second before a fist slammed into the side of her face. Lightning shot behind her eyes as the ground rushed up to meet her. Foliage and cool, damp earth plastered against her skin. How? How had he gotten through the woods without her noticing? The black ski mask she'd memorized the moment she'd met him slowly came into focus.

"I didn't want to have to do that, Madison, but you're not cooperating at all as I expected." Her attacker's knees popped as he crouched beside her. Brushing a section of her hair out of her face with a gloved hand, he fisted a chunk in his grip and forced her to meet his gaze. "Now the medical examiner is going to be able to tell you were hit in the face, and my whole plan of making your jump from the falls look like a suicide won't be believable. I guess if your body is tossed around a few times, she won't be able to tell the difference. Either way, you're off the Rip City Bomber case."

That was what this was about? That she'd been

the prosecutor assigned by the district attorney's office to try the case? The DA had personally handed her the case six months ago with his full support, a career-changing case that would ensure she could raise this baby on her own. Only now, her attacker made it sound as though she'd been targeted because she'd stepped into the limelight.

The bomber hadn't wanted a mistrial from the charges the DA's office had brought against Rosalind Eyler. He'd triggered the bomb in the courthouse to designate a specific prosecutor at the helm, to get her out of the way. Madison locked onto his wrist with both hands to ease the pain spreading across her scalp, but she wasn't strong enough to loosen his grip. There was only one reason someone would go to these lengths to assign a certain prosecutor on the biggest case the state had seen in a decade. The same reason she'd taken on the case in the first place. To use it as a stepping-stone to district attorney when Pierce Cook retired. "You want me off the case so you can be the one behind the prosecution's table when Rosalind Eyler is sentenced."

The list of suspects she carried around in her head narrowed considerably but expanded with the possibility of seventy-two new names. One name for each of the deputy district attorneys in her office. Madison ran through all the prosecutors she'd worked with over the years. "And Harvey

Braddock was helping you until you detonated a thermite bomb in his garage to tie up loose ends."

A gut-wrenching amusement filtered into those light green eyes, and Madison braced for the next hit. Her hand brushed against something solid on the ground beside her as her abductor straightened. A phone. He must've dropped it and hadn't noticed it'd fallen from his coat when he'd crouched beside her. "Unfortunately for you, he wasn't the only loose end."

"Don't let the baby bump fool you." She swept the phone into her hand while keeping total eye contact with her attacker. It was an old but successful trick she'd picked up from her father when he'd asked her to be the lookout at the convenience stores around their house. "I'm not going to make this easy for you."

Chapter Eight

There was no way to track her location.

Jonah had confiscated her phone at the court-house and taken the battery out to keep the bomber from being able to follow her movements. A lot of good that'd done. He'd been the one to bring her out in the open.

He brushed through the shattered glass over the passenger side of the SUV, his instincts on high alert. He had to catalog everything. No matter how small. One piece of evidence was all it would take to tell him who'd put his hands on the mother of his baby. Her tablet pencil stood stark white against the leather of the seat. She must've been working on her tablet when the attacker had surprised her by knocking out the window, but where was it? He hauled her bag from the floorboards and emptied the contents onto the seat. Wallet, car keys for a vehicle he was pretty sure didn't exist anymore, perfume, various shades of lipstick, a brush. "It's not here."

Her abductor wouldn't have taken the device. All the marshals service would've had to do was ping the tablet's whereabouts to narrow in on his location. Jonah ran his hand down between the middle console and the seat. And hit something solid. Tugging the tablet from the depths, he tipped the screen toward him, but was immediately denied access due to facial recognition. A nine-button keypad appeared on the screen. Madison hadn't dropped the tablet when she'd been attacked. She'd hidden it. Why?

Marshal Dylan Cove searched the back seats, the pavement, behind the vehicle, any possible angle their suspect might've approached the vehicle. "I'm coming up empty. You?"

"She hid her tablet between the console and her seat. There's something on here she thought was important enough to make sure I found when I discovered she'd been taken." Jonah slammed the door closed behind him harder than he'd meant. Someone had broken into his vehicle, had put their hands on Madison and taken her from the scene. And it would be the last thing they did in this life. "The company who makes these is well-known for not giving access to their customer's devices, especially to law enforcement. The tech experts won't be able to break into it in time, and I obviously don't look remotely like Madison. I need the passcode."

"Has to be something she uses every day." Cove unpocketed his phone. "I'll call the tech guys to see if they can pull keystrokes off of her work computer and laptop."

"She won't make it easy to guess. Not with confidential case files and documents from the district attorney's office." Which meant no birthdays, no social security numbers, nothing a hacker or opposing counsel could search personal information for to make a guess. "Three wrong entries will lock us out and wipe the memory. Damn it."

They were running out of time. Every minute she was out there was another minute her and the baby's lives were in danger, and he couldn't do a damn thing about it until he figured out the message she'd tried to leave behind for him. She was out there, alone, fighting for her life, and the thought of not finding her in time ripped the deep cuts in his heart wider. He'd already lost her once when she'd cut him from her life. He couldn't lose her again. The hollowness behind his sternum throbbed with the ticking clock. He brought the device up again, cursing the nine-button keypad. This wasn't going to work. He needed another angle, another—

Lines of light blue and white spread out from behind the numbered buttons on the screen followed by deep wells and curves of darker color that hadn't been there a moment ago. Small letters edged the perimeter of the background image. Madison's name, two separate dates, a gray scale and what looked like a bunch of numbers adding up to latitude and longitude. "Women's Healthcare Clinic."

The background photo wasn't a map. It was a sonogram of their baby. Jonah swiped at the screen to get the full picture. The outline of a small gray alien life-form curved around the bottom of the photo. A round head, perfect nose and full lips drew him in before he spotted the six-digit due date typed beside their son's feet. It was worth a shot. The longer they stood here, the higher the chance Jonah wouldn't get to Madison in time. Wouldn't get to his son in time. He tapped the screen to resurrect the keypad and punched in the due date.

The sonogram and keypad disappeared. A white document filled the screen. The Rip City Bomber case file at first glance with notes at the bottom in Madison's handwriting. He turned the device to get a better angle on three words underlined multiple times. "It's a setup."

Shock coursed through him, and he raised his attention to the scene where firefighters had finally extinguished the last of the thermite fires around Harvey Braddock's property. Forensic units had been given the go-ahead to assess the garage and start collecting evidence. All of it, this entire scene, had been made to look like Harvey Braddock had been involved in the attacks and had possibly made a mistake assembling a second bomb if the remains inside the garage turned out to be him, but Madison had figured it out. "She knew this device was to get me into the field and leave her unprotected before he came for her."

A ping registered from her tablet. An incoming message with an attachment. He didn't recognize the number, but that wasn't surprising. Madison had plenty of contacts, private investigators and law enforcement personnel she worked with on a daily basis. He tapped the attachment and a file filled the screen.

A photo of a location he recognized. He wasn't sure how to explain it, couldn't possibly convince anyone else, but his gut said the message had come from Madison. She must've gotten a hold of her abductor's phone. "Cove!"

Jonah wrenched open the driver's side door of his SUV and climbed inside. Dylan Cove collapsed into the passenger seat. In seconds, the engine growled to life. Jonah shoved the vehicle into Drive and ripped out of the neighborhood with a cloud of burnt rubber behind them. Grip tight on the steering wheel, he pushed past the legal speed limit as he wound between Portland traffic and headed toward the highway out of town. He tossed the tablet into Cove's lap, the photo from the unknown number stretched across the screen. "Multnomah Falls."

"You won't get there any faster if you're dead, Watson." Cove latched onto the handle above his head as Jonah wrenched the wheel to climb onto the highway on-ramp in front of another car.

"Watch me." Tires on asphalt droned in his ears, but his head was far from the miles of road in front of him. He should've known the thermite explosive had been set up to lure him and Madison to the scene. He should've seen it before now. Madison had. Right before the bastard had abducted her.

A deep well of desperation honed his senses into hyperfocus. He'd already lost one child because he hadn't been there. He couldn't lose another, couldn't lose Madison. This wasn't just about the pregnancy or his fear of reliving the past. These past eighteen hours of her falling under his protection, of having her this close, had resurrected those first tendrils of feelings he'd closed himself off from when Noah had died. She'd done that. She'd helped pull him above the secrets of his past and breathe renewed love and excitement into the life they'd created together. Something he'd never imagined he'd feel again. Without her, he would've drowned in the hollowness Noah's death had left behind, and he wasn't going to let anyone take her from him. Ever.

"The trailhead to the lower falls is up ahead."

Cove unholstered his weapon, checking the safety. "The photo was taken close to the bridge over the falls. If he's got her higher up the rocks, he'll see us as soon as we hit the trail. What's your plan here?"

"You take the main trail. I'll come up through the trees on the south. We can cover more ground that way, but believe me, if I know Madison, she'll make damn sure we know where she's at." Jonah pulled the SUV over and slammed the vehicle into Park. His boots hit the ground, and he brought his sidearm up. The heaviness of the steel tugged on the wound in his shoulder, but he bit back the pain. He couldn't afford any more mistakes. Not with Madison's life in the balance. Cool mist settled against his neck and face as he and Cove closed in on the trailhead.

Elongated shadows stretched across the dirt trail. The sun was setting. Five—ten—more minutes at the most and they'd lose the small amount of light outlining the path in front of them. Jonah slowed, crouching behind the largest rock blocking his view to the river. The steady rush of the falls drowned out any other sounds around them. The perfect location for an ambush. High sight lines, spotty reception, plenty of trees and rock for cover. So different from the bare landscape of Afghanistan. No sign of their bomber or Madison along the higher rocks or on the bridge, but that didn't mean they weren't out here. Radios wouldn't do them any good. They'd have to revert to signals.

Her message had come through a little more than thirty minutes ago. Was he already too late? Unclipping his phone from his vest, he brought up the trail map of the area. Jonah tapped Cove on the shoulder from a few inches behind the marshal. He motioned to the slick, well-worn main trail with two fingers, then nodded his intentions to take up the lesser-known path approximately fifty feet to the south of where they were standing.

Cove understood and fell into a steady pace along the main trail while Jonah diverted to the south. Thick trees and roots would slow him down, but nothing would stop him from getting to Madison. He headed straight into the trees with the trail map fresh in his head. If he hiked farther up the incline in this direction, he should hit the lower falls bridge before Cove's hike from the main trail. His boots sank a few inches at a time as he wound through overgrown trees and dead branches. His lungs burned with exertion with the added weight of his vest, but he pushed forward. He had to get to her. That was all that mattered.

A scream pierced through his loud breathing, and he locked on movement from the bridge. Two figures shifted through the trees, and Jonah pumped his legs as fast as they could go up the side of the mountain. "Madison!"

Twenty feet. Ten. He was almost there.

"Jonah!" His name tearing from her throat out of fear rocketed his pulse into his throat. She twisted out of her abductor's arms from the center of the bridge and took one step toward him as Jonah burst from the tree line.

Just before her attacker pushed her over the edge.

GRAVITY DUG ITS CLAWS into her muscles.

Madison reached for the marshal she'd trusted to save her a split second before her kidnapper pushed her over the side of Benson Bridge. The tops of the trees ringed her vision as she stared up in the sky, her scream cut off by the thundering beat of the falls six hundred feet below.

Seconds distorted into a full minute as the world slowed. She was falling, with no chance of survival once she hit the river.

"No!" Jonah had been running toward her, but he'd been too late.

She stretched out both hands, her fingers skimming down cold steel and concrete as panic charged through her. Her fingers spasmed at contact of the inner arch beneath the bridge, and Madison latched on for dear life. She'd caught herself. Her bare feet swung beneath the bridge—back and forth—as momentum and gravity combined forces to pull her free. The edge cut into her hand as she tried to adjust her grip on the frame, but she wouldn't be able to hold on for long. She wasn't strong enough. Her bulging belly brushed against the girder as she set her head back between her arms. Hot tears slipped down her face and into her hairline, immediately cooling with the help of the wall of water below her. "Jonah!"

The sob clawing up her throat was swept away in the rush of freezing water. He couldn't hear her, couldn't see her without looking directly over the bridge. There were two other arches to her right. If she could swing her feet onto one of them, she could slide across the girder to the rocks on the other side.

Her fingers were losing friction as water collected on the underside of the bridge. She adjusted her grip, kicking wildly to push momentum up her body and into her hands. Reverberations pounded through her from the bridge. She stared straight up and caught sight of two outlines throwing fists as the sun dipped beyond the horizon. Shadows chased across her vision from the dwindling light.

Jonah landed a hard right kick to her attacker's chest, forcing the masked bomber who'd taken her toward the center of the bridge. He blocked an incoming kick to his shin but failed to dodge the solid punch to the right side of his face. Her abductor followed through with an elbow into Jonah's head, and her marshal slammed into the side of the bridge above her. "Madison, hang on! I'm coming for you!"

Her abductor's shadow solidified behind the marshal. Dying sunlight glinted off a small piece of steel.

"Jonah, look out!" Her right hand tensed around the steel support girder as she loosened her left to reach for him, but she couldn't reach him.

Jonah straightened, his head thrown back onto his shoulders, as the steel disappeared into his side. His guttural scream cut through the constant pound of water on rock below and echoed off the rocks around her.

"No!" Her blood ran cold as he stumbled back, out of sight. Madison blinked through the mist of water sticking to her face, but she couldn't see him. "Jonah!"

One hand slipped from the girder, and the whole left side of her body plunged to drop. The phone she'd taken from her abductor fell from her pocket and disappeared into the raging waters below. Jonah was hurt. She had to get to the other side of the bridge. Her hand ached from the weight tensing her frozen fingers. She could do this. She had to do this. For Jonah. For her baby. She angled her head up toward the top of the girder and hauled her dislodged hand back into place. The tears dried as she focused every ounce of energy into sliding across the beam. Cold steel aggravated the cut at the base of her fingers as she pushed one hand over a few inches, then followed it with the other.

The shape of the arch dipped down, and her fingers slipped along the wet metal until she hit the divider built between the arches. Her heart shot into her throat, but she'd managed to slide a few feet closer to the edge of the rocks.

Two feet of steel separated her from the next arch to her right. She'd have to move one hand at a time and pray she was strong enough to hold on.

Heavy footsteps pounded across the bridge, and she looked up in time to see a third shadow separate from the tree line and collide with her attacker. "Watson, get to Madison! I'll hold him off!"

Recognition flared as Marshal Dylan Cove caught the bomber around the middle and hauled him across the bridge, all the while taking hit after hit to the top of his spine. Another round of fists flew before they fell out of sight onto the other side of the falls, but she didn't hear Jonah respond. Had Cove been too late?

Her hands hurt, every muscle in her arms shaking under the pressure. She had to keep moving, had to get to him—

"Maddi, take my hand!" His command claimed every cell in her body as Jonah stretched over the side of the bridge and down toward her. Crystal-clear blue eyes targeted her with nothing but determination, and a flood of sobbing relief washed through her. He was alive. He was going to get her out of here. "You can do this. I know you can do this."

Madison increased the pressure on her right hand—her dominant—in hopes of taking advantage of the added strength, but her fingers immediately slipped from the steel. She held on with her weakest hand as desperation lightninged through her veins. The tendons in her wrists ached, threatening to give out at any moment. She couldn't hold on much longer. One wrong move and she'd be lost to the falls forever. Her arm spun in the socket as her body swung away from the bridge. "Jonah!"

"Hang on, Maddi. I'm coming for you." His words were drowned from the gush of the rapids below. He disappeared from above her, and desperation turned to outright fear. He was going to try to get to her from the mountain of jagged black rocks and overgrown trees leading up to the bridge from the river, but she was still too far from the wall.

"Please." Numbness climbed into her fingers as circulation cut off due to her added weight. She still had to clear the divider before Jonah would be able to reach her, and it was now or never.

Vibrations rumbled beneath her grip as the fight on the deck of the bridge went into overtime, but she couldn't focus on Marshal Cove and her abductor right then. She was going to die if she didn't get across the underside of the bridge. She kicked out in order to face the steel girder once again. Her shoulder screamed in protest as she engaged muscles she felt like she hadn't ever used to shorten the space between her free hand and the other side of the divider, but she slowly inched her hand to the top of the girder. Latching on, she ignored the discomfort of the steel pressing into the top of her belly and locked her jaw against the pain tearing through her back.

The trees to her right bounced as Jonah climbed out onto a small ledge created by the natural erosion of the falls. Water gushed across his boots and the bottoms of his jeans, but right then it seemed he had attention only for her. "I'm right here, Maddi. I've got you. You're going to be okay. Just a little farther, and you'll be in my arms."

A little farther. That was all. Madison tried to convince her left hand to lift from the steel, but her right hand was already slipping down the arch of the second girder. She couldn't move. Not without letting go completely. There was nowhere for her to go but down. "I can't. There's too much water to get a grip."

"You're going to have to jump to me," he said.

He was insane. "I can't hold on any longer."

"Maddi, look at me." The compulsion in his voice dived deep past skin and muscle, straight into her bones to where she didn't feel she had a choice but to do as he asked. "You didn't come this far to throw it all away now. I know you're tired. I know you're hurting, but you are the strongest, most intelligent and most stubborn woman I've ever known. I want our son to grow up knowing his mother doesn't just put bad guys behind bars but that she stares fear in the face and tells it to go to hell. I want you to be the one he looks up to when he gets older, but to do that, you're going to have to jump to me."

"Okay." She nodded, more trying to convince herself than agreeing to his plan, but she didn't have any other choice. Not if she wanted to get out of here alive. If she released her left hand and held on to the girder with everything she had with her right, she could swing herself toward him. And trust him to catch her. "Okay."

"That's it." Jonah braced to catch her.

Prying her left fingers from the steel, she held her breath as she swung down and to the right, and at the last second released her hold altogether. Momentum propelled her straight toward Jonah, but she was dropping too fast. She hadn't created enough of a swing to thrust her onto the rocks. Madison reached out for him, the world threatening to slow again as gravity took control.

Jonah latched onto her wrist. "Gotcha!"

Her feet dangled freely above the rapids as she craned her head to look up at her rescuer. The veins in his arm battled to escape from the pressure of holding on to her. Jonah hauled her up and secured her in the circle of his arms, and she collapsed into him. Minutes had felt like hours as death had closed in, but against his chest, time sped up. "I've got you, Maddi. You're safe."

"Thank you." She set her forehead against his chest, reveling in the rhythmic beat of his heart. Tremors racked through her, and he hugged her closer. Right where she needed to be. "You're hurt. I saw him stab you."

"A blade wasn't going to stop me from getting to you," he said.

A scream echoed off the rocks around them, and Madison twisted her gaze up to the bridge's deck. "Marshal Cove."

Jonah's grip tightened around her. "Come on."

They raced up the rocky incline and curved around the edge of the bridge. Hand secure in hers, Jonah maneuvered her behind him, using himself as a shield against the abductor who'd tried to kill her. Both Marshal Cove and Jonah faced off with the masked kidnapper. "Your sick game is over, you bastard, and you're going to pay for every life you've taken these last few days, including the attempted murder of a deputy district attorney."

A deep laugh punctured through the exhaustion dragging Madison down now that she wasn't struggling to save her own life. "The game isn't finished, Marshal. Not by a long shot."

Her abductor threw himself over the side of the bridge.

Chapter Nine

Bright lights and pain increased the pressure at the back of his skull as the emergency room attending stitched the hole in his side. Jonah set his head back on the uncomfortable pillow and squeezed the edge of the mattress. He bit back a groan as the doc threaded the needle through the edges of his wound again. No painkillers. Nothing that would impede his decision-making and reflexes. There was too much at stake since he'd nearly lost Madison over the side of that damn bridge. He held his breath against the next wave as his stomach churned. "Any sign of him?"

"PPB hasn't come up with anything yet. No body. Not a single shoe to go off of. Remi is coordinating with Search and Rescue and their canines to see if the SOB managed to survive." Deputy Dylan Cove's voice softened at the mention of their chief deputy, but Jonah let it slide. Cove iced the split in his lip in his corner of the curtained section of Providence Point Medical Center's ER. Setting the ice pack in his lap, he tested the swelling with his free hand. "Who the hell throws themselves six hundred feet into freezing water like that?"

"Someone with a death wish, and when I find him, his wish is going to come true." Jonah tried to relax as the attending sewed the last stitch into place and wiped the area clean of blood. He tugged his shirt into place after a fresh piece of gauze had been taped over his side. The attending slipped out of the curtained-off area, leaving him and Cove alone. "Whoever he is, he's dangerous. Not only to Madison but also to civilians. He's already set off three bombs and killed nine people. Who knows what else he has planned."

"You make it sound like our bomber survived that fall." The marshal looked a little worse for wear than when they'd started their hunt for Madison at the Multnomah Falls trailhead, but if it hadn't been for the deputy who'd let her slip out of his protection before, Madison wouldn't be here. Jonah owed him.

"I'm not going to discount the possibility." No matter how slim the chances Madison's abductor had survived that fall, Jonah wouldn't take the risk of letting his guard down. Not until he was sure. He swung his legs over the side of the bed, the muscles around his shoulder reminding him to take it slow. "Have any of the victim statements, interviews of employees from the courthouse or neighbors around the second scene given us any new leads?"

"Considering I was getting knocked around by a masked bomber on the deck of that bridge, I wouldn't know. Forensics got their hands on the abductor's vehicle abandoned outside the trailhead, but so far they've only confirmed it was reported stolen three days ago. Last I heard, Reed and Foster were still canvassing Harvey Braddock's neighborhood on foot to see if anyone noticed suspicious activity. I'll check with them and the local cops for updates as soon as this room stops spinning." Cove pushed to his feet, ice pack at his side as he rubbed his bristled jaw. Bruising had already developed across the swollen section of his cheek where Jonah had punched him at Harvey Braddock's property. "Where's Madison? Hard to believe you'd leave her side after what went down."

"I had Remi take her to get checked out by Madison's doctor on the third floor while I got stitched up, and make sure everything is okay with the baby." His insides still hadn't gotten the message she was safe. They were coiled so tight it was hard to breathe.

"Aren't you supposed to be there for that?" Cove asked.

He wanted to be. He wanted to make sure she was okay, that their son was okay. Wanted to hear the heartbeat and see the life they'd created kicking on the ultrasound monitor. All the things he hadn't gotten to do when Noah's birth mother had been pregnant with him, but the fact Madison had gone out of her way to ensure she would be the sole parent to their son knotted a thick band of hesitation inside. She'd spent the past five months keeping Jonah at arm's length. A few hours of terror wouldn't change her mind. He wasn't sure anything could. A humorless laugh jarred the new stitches in his side, and he pressed his hand over the fresh gauze to keep the pain at bay as he set his feet onto the stark-white linoleum floor. "I'm pretty sure my face is the last thing she wants to see right now."

Someone had taken her right off a scene created to divide Jonah's attention and thrown her over bridge. He almost hadn't made it in time. If she hadn't grabbed onto the girders, she would've died right in front of him and taken their son with her. He'd promised to protect her, and he'd failed. An apology couldn't make up for that, yet part of him wanted nothing more than to be in that room to make sure she'd really survived.

"You won't know until you ask." Dylan Cove slapped Jonah below his injured shoulder, then disappeared beyond the curtain.

Jonah bit down on the sting exploding down his back. If the marshal hadn't been there to hold off

Madison's abductor while he'd rushed to pull her to safety, Jonah would've given him a matching bruise on the other side of Cove's face for that. But the deputy had a point. Assuming Madison wanted to shoulder on her own the emotional chain reaction of what she'd gone through was an excuse to protect himself against her constant rejection to be part of her life.

Sweeping the curtain aside, he located the elevators to the left and hit the ascend button. Within two minutes, the car settled on the third floor and the doors parted. He stepped out onto the maternity ward floor, the most secure in the building, and flashed his badge to the two nurses at the front station before moving through the double doors. Remington Barton stood outside one of the rooms farther down the hallway, and she immediately turned to face the possible threat. That was why he liked her. Always aware. Always prepared for the next threat. No matter where or who it came from. He motioned to her with his chin in greeting. "How is she?"

"Bruised, shaken, but she's holding it together." The chief deputy rested her right hand on her weapon as she studied the corridor before locking intense blue eyes back on him. "How's Cove?"

"Bruised, shaken, but he's holding it together." He couldn't stop the smile tugging at his mouth. Of all the marshals under her watch, she wanted to know about Dylan Cove first. "And here I thought you'd be worried about me."

"You can take care of yourself. Cove, I'm not so sure about. Good luck in there." Remi maneuvered around him, walking down the way he'd come. She'd made it only a few steps before she turned back. "Can I give you a piece of advice, Watson? Don't let this one go. She needs you more than she's letting on."

"Maybe you and Cove need to talk about your own problems instead of mine," he said.

With a fading smile, she gave him her back and headed down the hallway.

Jonah wrapped his hand around the door handle leading into Madison's hospital room. The past few hours had been the most desperate and terrorizing of his life. He set his forehead against the door, a soft, echoing rhythm reaching his ears. He pushed inside. His eyes adjusted to the dim lighting, instantly locking onto the bright glow of the monitor on the other side of the bed. Madison had pushed her shirt—torn and dirty—high above the roundness of her perfect belly. Resting both hands to her sides, she was the queen he'd built her up to be in his head. Stunning, regal. "Hey."

She turned caramel-colored eyes to him and smiled. "It's the heartbeat."

The obstetrician shifted the jellied wand over Madison's stomach and pointed at the screen. "And there's the heart. No sign of brain trauma or heart problems. You're going to have a completely healthy baby boy."

"No." Madison turned back toward the monitor. "We are."

The movement on the blue-and-black screen compelled Jonah to close the distance between them. He automatically sought her hand with his as he crouched beside Madison's bedside. Strong legs kicked out every few seconds on the monitor, insanely small fingers each outlined by thin lines of blue, and the tightness in Jonah's chest released. "That's our son."

"Everything looks great." The doctor hit a couple of more buttons before a roll of shiny white paper fed from the machine. She handed the sonograms to Jonah with a smile. "I'll give you two a few minutes. You're welcome to get dressed when you're ready, and I'll see you in a few weeks for our next appointment."

"Thank you," Madison said.

He wasn't sure if the obstetrician left, if she'd closed the door behind her or how long he sat there with the printouts in his hand. Jonah had focus only for the bandaged hand wrapped in his. Deep cuts crossed the undersides of her palms from holding on to the bridge. Because of him.

"You figured out the password to my tablet." She smoothed her thumb over the back of his hand in small circles.

"Our baby's due date. Didn't think your device could've fallen between the seats from a struggle. You had to have placed it there, which meant you were trying to tell me something before he took you." Jonah closed his eyes, the heat of rage stirring in his gut. "I'm sorry, Maddi. I almost lost you out there, on that bridge. If I'd gotten there a split second later—"

"You didn't." She pulled her hand from his and raised both of hers to frame his jawline. Forcing him to look at her, she brushed her fingers along his beard. "I'm here. I'm alive. The baby is okay. You saved us, Jonah, and not for the first time. There wasn't anything you could've done to stop him from taking me. Whoever he is, he's planned this from the beginning, and we've been one step behind."

He slipped his hand over her belly, feeling warmth and movement and every ounce of emotion he had left after the hell they'd been through. "I don't want to lose you again. Either of you."

Madison shifted across the bed and pulled him on the mattress beside her. Setting her head against his shoulder, she grazed her fingers down his arm. "You won't."

HE WAS ASLEEP beside her, and the big picture she'd had all these months of what the future would look like had slipped from her mind.

Madison studied the strong curve of his eyebrows, the shadows cast across his cheeks from long blond lashes, the perfect shape of his mouth that'd molded to hers so easily. They'd come straight from the hospital and collapsed into sleep, but the last time she'd been in this position—waking up beside him in a tumble of sheets—she hadn't realized she'd been pregnant. Now, with the fullness of her belly between them, his hand strategically conformed to the shape of her pregnancy, she was all too aware she'd made a mistake. She'd tried to keep him from being part of their son's life. Only if it hadn't been for him putting himself between her and that device at the courthouse or rushing to save her on that bridge, she wouldn't be here at all.

The rise and fall of his back, the ripple of muscles across his shoulders, gave credence to a leashed strength she'd never witnessed before those horrifying minutes on the bridge. He lay facedown, his pillow forgotten on the edge of the bed. Reaching out, she lightly traced the patch of gauze on his bare shoulder, and her insides clenched with awareness. Heat seared her fingers and burned through her veins, but the attraction between them had changed over the past few days. Deepened. Strengthened. Chased back the nightmares.

He'd been stabbed fighting for her life, yet the pain had slid from his features in sleep. No investigation. No life-or-death scenarios. No resentment for how their child would be raised between them. Right here, in this bubble they'd created away from reality, it was the two of them. She couldn't remember the excuses she'd created to keep her from putting herself in her mother's position as she studied him. Leaving her raw, vulnerable and exposed.

"That tickles." One startling blue eye opened, but she didn't pull her hand away. He'd brought her back to the cabin in the mountains, a stronghold against the outside world, but that didn't protect her from the danger gripping her heart in a vise. Didn't stop her from stupidly wanting more than this…arrangement between them. "How long have you been staring at me?"

"I lost track of time. For a while there, I thought you were dead." His laugh rumbled through the mattress and past her defenses, raising goose bumps on the backs of her arms. She brushed his hair off his forehead and revealed a darkening bruise at his temple. Jonah had come for her when she'd lost hope in those last moments before her attacker had thrown her over the bridge. She shouldn't have been surprised, but the thought of a man—her father—helping anyone but himself had colored her vision for so long. It almost made her feel as though the marshal who'd taken her into protective custody had done it for her. Not out of desperation to keep himself from losing another child or failing his assignment. Made her feel as though he cared. "I didn't want to move in case I woke you, but now I can't feel my legs, and I have to go to the bathroom."

"Okay." He pushed his hands into the mattress to sit up and turned toward her. Reaching for her, he gripped the long length of her outer thigh through the sweatpants she'd borrowed from him earlier and increased the pressure along her sore muscles. He massaged the aching muscles running down her legs. "Well, I can only help with one of those things."

As good as it felt to have him touch her, to care for her, to put her first, Madison pulled her knees up into her chest. "Jonah, stop. You don't have to keep pretending you're in this for more than the baby we made together."

"What are you talking about?" His hand settled against her leg, those brilliant blue eyes sharper than a minute ago.

"You used yourself as a shield to protect me from the bomb in the courthouse, and you raced to get to that bridge in time before I went over, but it wasn't for me, was it?" She smoothed her hand over her belly and lowered her chin toward her chest. "It was for him. Because you didn't want to lose him, and I understand why. I can't imagine how much pain and grief you've gone—"

Jonah crushed his mouth to hers. His tongue breached the seam of her lips, and she gasped as her entire body caught fire. This. This was what she'd needed to cut herself off from the dark, cruel reality waiting for them outside these walls. She'd needed this kiss. She'd needed him.

His fingertips dug into the side of her thigh, keeping her grounded and on cloud nine at the same time. She kissed him back with a wild desperation she hadn't let herself feel in so long, granting him access to the deepest, most self-conscious parts of her. He hiked her knee over his hip to bring them closer, but all too soon, he was pulling away.

Her pulse raged out of control. Her body screamed in protest as he put a foot of space between them, but she forced herself to remove her nails from his muscled back.

"Let me make one thing clear, Counselor. I want you. I've always wanted you, and the moment that bastard abducted you, I was set on killing him for putting your life in danger. Him and Marshal Cove for being stupid enough to leave you to protect yourself." He cocked his head to the side, sliding his hand beneath the edge of her oversize shirt to graze his fingers along her belly. "We're having a son together, Maddi, but he doesn't detract from what I feel for you. What I've always felt for you. Nothing could. If anything, he's only made me want you—what we had before you took that pregnancy test—more."

Shock stilled the air in her lungs. "You didn't put yourself between me and that bomb because you were afraid of losing him?"

"I won't lie to you. That thought, and all the anger and fear I felt when I lost Noah, crossed my mind, but I did it because I couldn't stand the thought of losing you, too," he said. "All those late nights in your office were some of the best times of my life, but having you here in the cabin in which I intended to raise my family far outweighs the pain I went through when my son passed away. I'll never forget his loss and how his death drove me to join the marshals service, but I can't only hold on to the bad parts of my past. I have to be able to focus on the good parts, too, and that's where you come in."

Wow. She didn't... She didn't know what to say to that. Didn't know how to feel. He cared about her. Not the fact she was carrying his baby but her, and her heart rate picked up a bit more. Madison brushed her thumb across his bottom lip where the skin had darkened after the battle with her abductor on the bridge. She hadn't had anyone fight for her before—choose her—especially not her parents unless her existence managed to get them a larger payout from the government. She wasn't sure how to process the intensity in his expression or where to go from here. She dropped her hand away from his mouth. She'd devoted her entire life to planning for the future, of being independent from everyone, but whatever this was between her and Jonah didn't fit into that plan. What did that mean? "Those were some of my best nights, too."

"Glad to hear it." His smile lit up her insides before he rolled away and sat up on the edge of the king-size mattress. The wound in his side seemed to slow him down, but a sound never left his mouth. Always trying to stay in control, dependable, strong. To pretend the pain didn't get to him. "You should go back to sleep. I need to check in with my division. I'll see if there are any developments from the courthouse or Harvey Braddock's property and check the security system."

She had experience with the need to soldier on, no matter the circumstances. Then she'd been thrown over a bridge because her abductor had wanted her gone from behind the prosecution's table in the Rip City Bomber trial. Curling her battered fingers into fists, she closed her eyes against the onslaught of panic and fear clawing up her throat. Light green eyes flashed to the forefront of her mind. She hadn't recognized her attacker. Not his build. Not his voice. Not the pieces of his face she'd caught glimpses of as she'd struggled to get free of his grip on that bridge. "Police haven't found a body, have they?"

"Search and Rescue took their canines along the trail to see if they could pick up a scent, but no.

No body." He looked at her from over his shoulder but didn't fully face her. "I've got all available officers looking to find him, but with the power of the falls, I'm not sure they ever will."

"Were the tech guys able to trace the phone I used to send the message to my tablet?" If they could trace it back to the seller, that might lead them to wherever the man in the mask had purchased it. They might recover security footage.

"It was a burner, one serial number off from the phone used to take credit for the bombing at the courthouse. Purchased at the same time from the same seller, but when PPB investigated, they found out the security footage hadn't worked for months." Finally, Jonah turned, nothing but guilt and regret contorting his features. "I'm sorry, Maddi. I gave you my word I'd protect you, and when it counted the most, I wasn't there. I left you with Cove because I thought he'd keep you safe, but I should've been there. I should've…"

Her stomach clenched. Lifting herself onto her knees, she crawled across the bed. She wrapped her arms around him from behind and pressed her heart against his back. "Jonah, what happened at Harvey Braddock's house wasn't your fault. You know that. Whoever's behind these bombings, whoever is trying to kill me, has planned every step of this mind game in advance. We're just the pawns."

"You're right. We are just pawns." Jonah lowered his mouth to her arm, planting a soft kiss to her oversensitized skin. He turned into her, and she sat back on her heels. Determination chased back the agony in his expression. "We need to talk to the queen."

Chapter Ten

Jonah had been working this entire investigation with one arm tied behind his back. The bar door ahead of him slid back with a hard thrust as an overhead buzzer alerted the guards of movement. Shiny white tile reflected his and Madison's outlines and the fluorescent lights from above back up to him as they were escorted by the prison's warden into the cell block corridor.

"She's been waiting for you." The warden, the most no-nonsense woman he'd ever met, cast her gaze into each cell as they passed. "Said you'd come crawling to her sooner or later."

"Then she's as delusional as I thought." Women of varying ages, hair colors and rap sheets all wore the same bright orange uniform assigned to them after they'd been sentenced. One by one, Jonah walked past the cells, haunted gazes and violence in the inmates' expressions, and he had to battle the urge to reach for Madison.

She didn't need him to fight her battles. She'd gone up against plenty of monsters in court and come out on the other side stronger and more determined, and right then, he couldn't afford to let his emotions get in the way of keeping her alive. Not when they were about to interrogate a serial bomber who'd been keeping secrets to herself.

The warden paused outside a thick steel door with a slice of window cut into the middle. Through the double-paned glass, a monster stared back from the table in the center of the room. "She's handcuffed to the table, but don't underestimate her. Rosalind Eyler is one of the most dangerous inmates I've ever had the displeasure of holding in my prison. She's under twenty-four-hour surveillance by a guard at all times. When you're done, let him know."

"Twenty-four-hour watches are for inmates who've tried to escape." Jonah's fingers tingled for his weapon, but jail policy had forced him to leave it at the gate.

"If I know anything about Rosalind Eyler, she's been looking forward to this conversation as much as we have." Madison nodded and pulled her shoulders back, accentuating the line of her fresh maternity dress. "Open the door."

The warden signaled to the watch commander.

The buzzer echoed down the corridor once again, and the heavy steel door swung wide. Madison stepped inside first, Jonah right behind her, and they moved toward the table in the center of the bare concrete room.

"I was wondering how many people had to die before you came to see me. What is the body count up to now? Eight or nine?" The Rip City Bomber accentuated the laugh lines etched into the sides of her mouth with a close-lipped smile as Jonah slid the chair out for Madison, then took his own seat. "Always the gentleman, isn't he, Madison? Probably puts your needs before his own. Nothing like the men who plagiarized my research to advance their careers."

"You know we're not here to talk about Marshal Watson, Rosalind." Madison set her tablet between her and the bomber and swiped through the crime scene photos the bomb squad had taken of the courthouse, Madison's destroyed vehicle and Harvey Braddock's home. "I want to talk about the bomber who has taken credit for three bombings in the Rip City Bomber's name. Do you recognize his work?"

The smile vanished. The corner of Rosalind's left eye twitched slightly, something Jonah would've missed completely if he hadn't been looking for it, and he fought to keep himself from smiling. Rosalind Eyler wasn't happy the spotlight had shifted from her. The Rip City Bomber locked deep green eyes on him, and the hairs on the back of his neck stood on end. This woman had been responsible for the death of thirty-two victims in the last year, and there wasn't a hint of remorse in her expression. She wasn't just a bomber. She'd become a serial killer. "Do you know what the best part of being caught has been, Marshal Watson? Getting to relive every detail of what I did to my colleagues during the trial. It takes a lot to surprise the cops and investigators, but the families? I could live off seeing their pain for the rest of my life."

Rage coiled hot and bubbling in his gut. Rosalind Eyler wouldn't help them. She'd just wanted an audience. Jonah pushed back in his chair and focused on Madison. "We're done here."

"I think you're right." The deputy district attorney gathered her tablet from the table and stood to follow his retreat. They'd made it halfway across the room before another word left the inmate's mouth.

"Wait." Rosalind's voice spiraled tension down his spine.

Jonah and Madison turned in tandem to face the Rip City Bomber. Waiting.

"Show me the photos of the device from the courthouse." Rosalind leaned back in her chair as far as she could with her wrists cuffed to the table in front of her, her bright red hair nearly blending in with the red of her uniform. "I promise to behave."

He nodded to Madison, and they made their way back to the table. Retaking her seat, Madison scrolled through the photos sent from the bomb squad showing off the key components collected into evidence. Bits and pieces of the explosive charge, the switch, fuse, container and the power source draped against a light blue cloth. Jonah recognized each component for what it was, but the process in which individual bombers built their creations was unique. "The first two devices were remotely triggered to detonate with a cell phone using ammonium nitrate as the charge. The same setup you used in the four bombs you set off a few months ago. The third utilized thermite and ammonium nitrate to try to convince us Harvey Braddock is involved when it exploded on his property."

"You're right, Marshal Watson." Those empty green eyes studied the photo on the screen. "Whoever took credit for this device certainly has done their homework, but they missed one vital piece of the puzzle. I made all of my ammonium nitrate from scratch in my lab, and from the looks of it your bomber went straight to an ice pack."

No concern for Harvey Braddock. Interesting.

"An ice pack?" Madison asked.

"Cold packs are designed with two bags inside, one with ammonium nitrate and the other with water. When you break them open, the two bags mix and cause an endothermic reaction that absorbs heat." Jonah kept his gaze on the killer in front of him. The slight difference in the explosive charge wasn't nothing, but it wasn't the information he'd hoped to learn from the Rip City Bomber either. "We were able to trace the ammonium nitrate Rosalind used in her bombs to her lab because she'd made it herself. Whereas, an ice pack purchase is impossible to trace."

"Unless you know where to look." Rosalind cut her attention to Madison.

His instincts kicked in, and Jonah leaned forward to set his elbows on the table. What the hell did that mean? "You know who's behind these attacks."

Rosalind did the same, leaning across the table. The smile was back as the Rip City Bomber slid her gaze to Jonah. "Have you two picked a name already?"

Jonah didn't answer. He wasn't giving this psychopath an ounce of personal information, no matter what she thought she knew about him or Madison. He was here for information about the bomber who'd abducted the woman beside him. Not to play games. "How did the bomber know what components you used in your devices? That information wasn't made public."

"You're still not sure how you feel about him." Rosalind spoke to Madison as pressure built behind Jonah's sternum. Fluorescent lighting darkened the freckles clustered around her nose and forehead. "You worked so hard to get where you are, all without the help of the people who were supposed to care about you. I bet it's hard to forget all the pain and isolation from your childhood, even harder to let someone get close again. After all, he could be like your father."

Stiffness knotted at the base of Jonah's spine.

"You don't know what you're talking about." The muscles along Madison's jawline ticked every few seconds, her voice dropping to a whisper. Her fingers tightened around the tablet pencil in her hand, her knuckles white.

"Don't I?" Rosalind's eyes grew distant. The chains around her ankles dragged softly against the cement. "You and I aren't so different, Deputy District Attorney. We're both high achievers determined to rise above our circumstances. You in law, me in science. Our entire lives, men have used and abused us for their own gain. My father used me the same as yours used you, and now we're each having to deal with the effects of that trauma by relying only on ourselves. By shutting everyone out who could be a threat to our independence. The only difference is that I had the courage to make sure no one ever took advantage of me again when I killed my colleagues in those explosions. Can you say the same?"

Madison didn't answer.

Jonah's hands shook beneath the table. Rosalind Eyler was nothing like the woman sitting next to him. For every innocent life the Rip City Bomber had taken, Madison had saved lives one hundred times over by putting criminals like Rosalind behind bars. "I'm only going to ask you one more time. How did the bomber know what components you used in your devices?"

Slowly, Rosalind slid her wrists to one side of the table. Her long-drawn-out inhale filled his ears. "Because I told them. It's a shame he couldn't follow simple instructions, though. If he'd angled the device toward the courtroom instead of the outside wall as I'd told him, he'd have gotten exactly what he wanted and so would I."

"What you wanted?" Confusion rippled through him as he studied the woman sitting across from them. They hadn't been able to make a physical connection between the bomber and Rosalind Eyler, but his instincts had proved to be right. The Rip City Bomber knew who'd triggered the explosion at the courthouse and Harvey Braddock's home, who'd tried to kill the mother of his unborn child. Heat flared up his neck and into his face. His voice dipped into dangerous territory. "You made a deal with the bomber before the preliminary hearing. Who is it?"

"Oh, no, Marshal Watson. We're not even close to finishing this game." The bomber sat up straight, an injection of lightness and humor slipping across her expression. The handcuffs at her wrists and ankles knocked against the steel table. "I've got a lot of years ahead of me here, and I quite like the company, but I was willing to make a deal with him so I'll make one with you."

"What kind of deal?" Madison asked.

"I'll tell you the location of your bomber's lab—" Rosalind Eyler smiled again "—if you publicly reduce the charges against me."

FRESH AIR HIT HER square in the chest as Madison stepped out of the SUV in front of Jonah's cabin. She worked to purge the last thirty minutes from her pores, but her mind kept spinning. What the hell had happened in that room? They'd come to the prison to get answers, but she and Jonah had left with only more questions than when they'd started. Rosalind Eyler had given the courthouse bomber the exact components she'd used in four previous devices around Portland and had made some kind of deal with him before the device had been triggered. All for her to give up his laboratory's location to investigators in the end?

It didn't make sense.

There were still pieces missing from this puzzle, and something deep inside warned Madison it'd be too late before she understood the big picture. She combed her hair back away from her face. Her boot heels sank deep into soft earth as she headed toward the front door. "This is all just a game for her. Rosalind Eyler's not giving up the laboratory's location out of the goodness of her heart. She knows she's looking at spending the rest of her life behind bars, and she wants to cause as much chaos as possible before we shove her in a dark corner and forget her name."

"Makes me wonder what kind of deal she struck with the bomber, and how the hell he was supposed to hold up his end with his partner behind bars. She gives him the list of components of her devices in exchange for what?" Jonah maneuvered around the front of the SUV and jogged to catch up with her. He slipped his hand between her rib cage and arm to keep her from slipping. "Keeping the Rip City Bomber's name alive and horrifying?"

Madison slowed before they reached the front door, her hand still wound around his arm. Interesting theory. "Rosalind never claimed she was innocent. Not from the moment she was arrested to when she was scheduled to appear at the hearing. What if making deal after deal gives her a way to relive the bombings, to see how many people she's hurt? You heard her in there. The Rip City Bomber is the kind of woman to feed off other peoples' pain. We're closing in on her partner, and maybe that's not acceptable to her. She wants to make the game last as long as possible. She wants to be recognized as the opponent she is, even if she has to do it from behind bars."

"You think her offer to lead us to the bomber's laboratory is another way to make the game last?" Soft puffs of air crystallized in front of Jonah's mouth in the high elevation, but the memory of how his mouth had taken hers in a flood of release stronger than she'd ever experienced before countered the chill.

"I think she'll do anything to hold on to the spotlight this trial has cast on her. No matter who she hurts in the process." Madison reached up, skimming her fingers along his jaw. His perfectly maintained beard bristled against her skin and shot a charge of desire through her. Ice blue turned into molten waves in his eyes before he caught her hand in his. Tingling sensations spread from where his thumb rubbed small circles into the back of her hand. "I just don't want you to be one of the people Rosalind hurts."

"I'm not going to let that happen." Keeping her hand in his, Jonah inserted the key into the front door and twisted. Warm air replaced the coolness prickling her skin as he pulled her inside. He tossed his keys onto the side table to their left, closed the door behind them and set the alarm panel in less than two breaths before tugging her into his chest. He slipped his hands to her hips, pressing her baby bump into his lower abdominals, and stared down at her. "I've already lost everything I cared about once and barely survived, Maddi. I'm going to fight like hell to make sure it never happens again."

She believed him. The grounding sensation of safety spiked through her as she lifted onto her toes and pressed her mouth to his. No matter how many times she'd pushed him away over these past five months, he'd never turned his back on her. Never gave up on her, on them. The tightness of his grip on her hips said he wouldn't start now. Electricity singed across her nerve endings with every stroke of his mouth against her, building a knot of frenzy inside.

She'd tried. She'd tried to keep herself from depending on someone else, but Jonah had made it so easy. He'd saved her life, put her needs above his own. He'd sacrificed his own desires to give her what she thought she wanted when it came to raising this baby on her own, and she'd fallen deeper into the trap. She'd started relying on him.

A rush of fear surfaced and vacuumed the air from her lungs. Everyone she'd ever relied on had disappeared. Her father, her mother when she'd died. Her friends, family. No one had stepped forward to fight for her. Rosalind Eyler and she did have one thing in common. In the end, Madison had to realize nobody would ever be coming to save her when she'd been a kid. She'd had to save herself, but the emptiness she'd tried to use as her greatest strength couldn't support her anymore. Not when Jonah had given her an anchor to hold on to, and every cell in her body revolted at the thought of losing him, too. She tangled her fingers in his hair and broke the kiss, out of breath. She needed to know, needed to hear the words. "Jonah, promise. Promise me you won't stop fighting for me. No matter what happens, don't give up on us."

Us. The concept of being tied to another person had scared her her entire life after what she'd witnessed her mother go through. Only now, that fear had transformed into something else entirely. Hope.

"I'll never stop fighting for you, Maddi. Never." He crouched, lowering his mouth to her throat, and hiked her legs around his waist. He headed toward the grand staircase leading to the bedrooms on the second level. Pale wood and neutral furnishings passed in a blur before he laid her across the end of the king-size bed of the master. Slower than she could stand, he slipped his fingers beneath her calves and unzipped her boots from top to bottom. They landed with a thud beside the bed, and he straightened, every inch the marshal she'd admired since the moment they'd met. Standing above her, Jonah ran his palms over her belly through the fabric of her dress. Small kicks from their son registered on one side. "You are so damn perfect. Why the hell would I ever stop fighting for you?"

She couldn't help but smile, setting her palms over his. "Because you know I'm out of your league."

"You got that right." His laugh charged through her, straight into her core, and her insides melted. Leveraging his hands on either side of her head, he brushed his mouth against hers. "Don't move a muscle."

How could she? He'd rendered her helpless in the best way imaginable. Madison sank into the mattress as the rush of water filled her ears. Steam tendrilled from the open doorway leading into the bathroom after a few minutes before cutting off abruptly, and she pressed into her elbows to sit up. "Jonah?"

Sleeves rolled up to expose strong forearms, he left the confines of the bathroom and reached for her. He took both of her hands in his and pulled her off the bed into the length of his body. "Turn around."

She narrowed her gaze on him. She didn't understand this game, but the deepest part of her—the one she'd ignored far too long—trusted him. Trusted he wouldn't hurt her. She turned in his arms, giving him her back. Heightened awareness overwhelmed her senses as he trailed a path of kisses along her neck from behind. He wrapped one hand around her front, cradling their son, while he tugged the zipper to her dress lower. Heated desire shot down her spine at the brush of his shirt against her bare skin. Cocking her head to one side, she gave him access to the most vulnerable parts of her. Physically. Mentally. Emotionally. Jonah Watson, the reserved, quiet, loyal marshal who'd put himself between her and the bomb at the courthouse, lit parts of her she'd cut herself off from feeling all these years, and the constriction in her chest loosened.

"You've held yourself together for so long, Maddi. You've spent your entire career taking care of everyone else. It's time you let someone take care of you for once." His whispers tickled the oversensitized skin of her neck and shoulders as he slipped her dress down her arms. Cool air rushed to replace the heat he'd generated beneath her skin as her dress fell in a pool at her feet. Leaving her in nothing but her bra and underwear—exposed—Jonah entwined his hand with hers and led her into the bathroom.

She followed ghostlike wisps of steam to the source, the large soaker tub he'd filled with full pink-tipped lotus flowers floating across the surface. Gravity worked to bring her to her knees as she took in the beauty of the added candles and colorful crystals positioned around the edge of the tub. Self-consciousness drained the longer she fought to speak. "When did you…" Her gaze cut to his as thick emotion stuck in her throat. No one had ever drawn her a bath before. No one had gone out of their way or seemed to care about her the way he did. "You did this for me?"

"You've spent nearly your entire life feeling unloved and forgotten, Maddi, but I never forgot you. No matter how many times you pushed, I couldn't walk away. You gave me something I didn't think I'd ever feel again after I lost Noah. You gave me hope for the future." He framed her face between calloused palms, stroking her cheeks with his thumbs. Blue eyes studied her from forehead to chin. "And I'll spend every day of the rest of my life proving I'm the one person who will never stop choosing you."

She couldn't think, couldn't breathe. Her lips parted as he pressed his mouth to hers in another adrenaline-inducing dizziness of desire. She fisted his shirt in her hands and pulled him toward the bathtub.

Chapter Eleven

Everything he'd ever wanted rested on the other side of the bed. Madison's long dark hair fell in silken waves over her pillow and framed the mesmerizing brush of pink in her cheeks. Night had fallen, only punctures of moonlight coming through the wall-to-wall windows stretching across the room. He wasn't sure how long they'd been lying there since he'd brought her back to bed. Didn't care about anything outside of these four walls, but reality wouldn't stop fighting for long.

As much as Jonah wanted to believe the bomber who'd thrown himself off that bridge hadn't survived the fall, his gut warned otherwise. The bombs at the courthouse, the thermite explosive at Harvey Braddock's house… Something he couldn't explain said the dive off the Benson Bridge had been part of the plan, and it was only a matter of time before the killer came for Madison again.

His phone vibrated from the dresser on the other side of the room. Careful not to wake Madison, he slid from the bed, leaving her exactly where she was supposed to be. He silenced the device as soon as he reached the dresser and stepped out into the hallway before answering. "Either you're up late, or you haven't gone to sleep either."

"Who needs sleep?" Remington Barton sounded as exhausted and wound up as Jonah did. The entire division had been called in to hunt for the bomber responsible for nine deaths in the past three days, and if he was a betting man, Jonah would say Remi hadn't wanted to let anyone else take point. "Did you get a chance to read through the bomb squad's report from the thermite fire at Harvey Braddock's home?"

"Give me a minute." He made his way downstairs and collapsed onto the couch. He pulled his tablet onto his lap. His vision battled with the sudden brightness from the screen before he opened the attached file in his email. His stomach rolled. "The body recovered from the garage was confirmed to be Harvey Braddock."

"You reported when you spoke to Rosalind Eyler, she'd revealed her exact components for the bombs she detonated over the past year to the bomber we're hunting, but the prison logs say she hasn't had any visitors aside from her attorney. No mail. No phone calls," Remi said. "I think we discovered how she was able to communicate to the outside."

"Her lawyer." Damn. He'd been afraid of that. Jonah leaned back into the couch. "Rosalind used Harvey Braddock as a go-between, then had her partner kill him and lure me away from Madison all in the same swing."

"She's not just intelligent, Jonah. She was the lead chemist working for the biggest pharmaceutical company in the country." Remi's voice faltered. "Putting her behind bars hasn't stopped her from finishing what she started, and for some reason she's deviated from her MO of working alone and put Madison Gray in her sights. I need you to watch your back."

"I will." The only other option was losing everything he'd fought for since starting the adoption process with Noah, and he couldn't go back to that life. Couldn't survive the isolation, the emptiness. Not after what he and Madison had been through. "I still don't understand how our perp was able to get onto that scene at Harvey Braddock's house. Local PD had the perimeter sealed off and were ID'ing everyone who crossed that line." Tension twisted his insides. "Unless…"

"Our bomber had the clearance to cross that line." Remi sighed. "I'll have Cove reinterview the officers assigned perimeter duty. See if he can pull anything out of the ordinary from their statements.

If our suspect is in law enforcement, they'll have access to everything concerning the investigation."

"That's how he's staying ahead of us." As much as Jonah hated to admit it, their new pool of suspects made sense. It explained how the bomber was able to get in and out of the courthouse during construction to plant the first device in the HVAC unit. It explained how he was able to step into and leave the second scene. It explained how the bastard had learned of Jonah's experience with thermite and his background in explosives. The pieces were beginning to fit. All that was left was to fill in the silhouette shadow at the back of his head with a face. Couldn't be any of the marshals from his team. Even with his desire to deck Dylan Cove again, Remi had vouched for the former private investigator on more than one occasion. Jonah trusted her, and he trusted her vetting process for bringing in new marshals. Both Finnick Reed and Beckett Foster had been at his side for the past decade. While the past six months had changed their lives drastically with Beckett's daughter on the way and a new wife on his arm, and Finnick head over heels with a new crime scene photographer who'd once been his witness, that left the PPB officers assigned to perimeter security. And one other person. "How well do you know the special agent who was at the Braddock scene?"

"I don't." Surprise notched Remi's voice up an

octave. "All I know is the Bureau assigned Special
Agent Jackson to support the local bomb squad
with the investigation. I figured you knew him
considering you both worked for the FBI's hazardous devices unit a good chunk of your life, and the
scene just hadn't been a great place to catch up.
It's not exactly a social situation."

"No. I've never met him before." He'd worked
with an entire team of agents—dozens from all
over the country and outside of it—but Jonah was
positive he'd never met Special Agent Collin Jackson in his life. Didn't mean the agent wasn't in
Portland on a valid assignment or that he'd lied
about his reasons for being on the scene, but Madison's life was worth finding out for sure. "I know
most of the agents still working in that unit. Where
is he now?"

"Here, at the Second Avenue station running
through the same report I sent you." The low hum
of voices and ringing phones filled the line. "He
confirmed the thermite found at the house and
the amount stolen from the warehouse two nights
ago are a match, and that Harvey Braddock is the
victim firefighters pulled from the garage. Agent
Jackson is trying to put the pieces of the device
from the garage back together. Hopefully we'll be
able to pull prints from one of the components to
get a lead on Rosalind Eyler's partner."

"Keep him there while I check into his background, Chief." Footsteps padded down the grand staircase behind him. Hell, he hadn't meant to wake her. "I'll check in with you in the morning."

"Jonah, wait," Remi said before he was able to hit End. "There's something else."

His heart beat steadily in his throat as he raised the phone back to his ear. "What is it?"

"Search and Rescue recovered a stash of clothing and a ski mask a few feet from a set of tracks leading up from the bank of the river." Silence grew heavy around him as Jonah waited for the fist around his lungs to ease. "I'm having forensics comb through the evidence, but preliminary tests have me convinced Madison's abductor survived that fall after all."

The nightmare wasn't over.

"Thanks for letting me know." He ended the call and craned his neck up to watch Madison stop at the bottom of the stairs. "Sorry. I didn't think I was talking loud enough to wake you."

"You weren't, but the bed got cold without you in it." She closed the distance between them, sliding onto his lap with one arm snaking behind his neck. He couldn't help but wrap her in his arms as she rested her head against his shoulder. Turning the tablet to face her, Madison scanned through the document. "The medical examiner identified the body recovered at the scene. Harvey Braddock was involved."

Shock wove between her words, and his stomach revolted. According to her, Madison and Harvey hadn't exactly been friends on opposites sides of the courtroom, but neither of them had had any real ill will toward the other. Not until now. "USMS believes he was acting as Rosalind Eyler's messenger between his client and the bomber, and when they didn't need him anymore…"

"They killed him." Her shoulders rose on a strong inhale, and before he had a chance to tighten his hold on her, she slipped from the circle of his arms. The tablet screen highlighted and shadowed the angles of her expression as she swiped through to the next page of the document, lost in the investigation. How many times had he watched her like this? Her with her focus drawn to the case in front of her, him waiting for her to come back to the present and remember he was there.

It'd been in quiet moments like this in the middle of the night in her office where she'd let him get to know the real her. Not the deputy district attorney trying to win the latest case thrown at her by the DA, but Madison. The woman who bit her bottom lip while analyzing the next pattern, who stayed up late and woke up early to fight for the innocent, who found little value in small talk and other social rituals and strangely remained calm in any situation. The woman who'd somehow broken through the numbness he'd carried all these years and made him feel again. Not just the good parts of life but the ugly, too. In less than three days, she'd untangled years of grief and rage tearing him apart from the inside and expected nothing in return. Hell, that was why he'd fallen in love with her.

His breath hitched. Love.

In an instant, Madison pegged him with caramel-brown eyes as though she'd sensed the realization that ripped the air from his lungs. She lowered the iPad to her side. "You told your chief to keep someone at the station while you look into his background before I came downstairs. You have a new suspect?"

"Special Agent Collin Jackson," he said.

"He would've had clearance to the courthouse during construction." Her outline shifted in the dark, the roundness of her baby bump catching the light from dying embers in the stove. Unsettled energy rolled her fingers into her palms. She seemed to want to pace, walk it out, talk this new theory through, but the attacks had taken too much from them both. "Could explain why he was able to get past the officers at the perimeter of the scene at Harvey Braddock's, but I don't recognize his name. As far as I know, he hasn't been involved in one of my cases before now. What makes you suspicious of an agent?"

"He told Remi he worked for the Bureau's hazardous devices unit, but I've never met him before either, and I don't recognize his name. That gives him opportunity and the know-how he'd need to build those devices." All of which was easy enough to confirm with a few calls, but it was only three in the morning in Washington, DC. His suspicions would have to wait until sunrise.

"You think he's lying," she said. "That he's the bomber?"

"I can't say for sure yet." Jonah pushed to his feet. He'd spent the past five months apart from her. He couldn't keep his distance anymore. "But I'm not discounting the possibility our perp is law enforcement, no. There's too much at risk to make that kind of mistake."

"There's only one problem with focusing solely on law enforcement." She turned the tablet screen toward him. "The police and the FBI aren't the only ones with access to this investigation."

"THE MAN WHO dragged me up to those falls wasn't interested in a mistrial for the Rip City Bomber case. He wanted me out of the way, but not to guarantee a win for Rosalind Eyler. I think he wants to prosecute the case himself." From the moment Jonah had pulled her off that bridge, she hadn't been able to slow down long enough to process what'd happened in that terrifying hour she'd been abducted. Only the soft sizzling of the dying fire in the stove reached her ears this late at night. Without aches bruising the muscles in her body and her head finally clear of the physical tension between her and Jonah, Madison had the headspace to analytically sink back into this case. Into her safe space. Her comfort zone. "There are seventy-three deputy district attorneys in Oregon, and every single one of their careers would change with a case like this on their résumé. We need to focus our efforts on them."

Embers cast dim orange shadows across Jonah's face as he stared down at her. Even in the dark, the concern etched into his expression picked her heart rate up. He'd done nothing but take care of her since the first bombing, despite the hell she'd put him through since she'd read that positive pregnancy test. "We've been operating under the assumption that the man who took you and the person who set off those bombs are one and the same. What if they aren't? What if there's another threat out there I haven't seen coming?"

"You haven't. My kidnapper specifically pointed out I should've died in that explosion, but I didn't. Because of you. No matter what happens, we both know you've done everything in your power to keep me safe. I trust that, and I trust you." She stepped into him as much as her swollen belly would allow and framed his jaw with both hands. "According to the caller taking credit for the bombing, the device in the courthouse was meant for me. I think without Search and Rescue finding a body in that river, we need to consider all the possibilities, but we've been looking for motive and now we have one. Narrowing our suspect pool to the other deputy district attorneys in the county gives us the bomber's motive for targeting me, explains how they could've gotten into the courthouse during construction and how they have continuous access to this investigation."

Silence settled between them as her theory became reality.

"You're right. They haven't found a body." Jonah seemed to tense right in front of her. "But they did find a stash of clothing hidden along the riverbank and footprints coming straight out of the water."

Air stalled in her lungs. Quick flashes of memory lightninged across her mind. The light green, hate-filled eyes of the man who'd taken her, the feeling of his hands on her arms as he'd tried to force her over the bridge. How much stronger he'd been than her, desperate. He was still out there, still hunting her. Whoever'd built those bombs was intelligent, adaptable and dangerous, and nothing like she'd gone up against before. "He must've had a change of clothes, maybe some supplies, waiting for him as part of his escape plan. He's never going to stop, is he? Not until I'm dead or I give up on everything I've ever worked for."

"He can't find you, Maddi. Nobody knows you're here. Not even my team." Jonah shifted between both feet and latched onto her arms. "I made sure of that when I took the battery out of your phone and put you into protective custody. Even with all the access this SOB has to the investigation and the connection he shares with Rosalind Eyler, he can't get to you."

"I hope you're right." She smoothed her hand over her hardening stomach. "For both of our sakes."

"I'll hold off on accusing Special Agent Jackson of terrorism and focus on the other deputy DAs, but I'm still going to talk to my unit back east and ask some questions about why he's here and why I've never heard of him." His hands drifted to her wrists, lightly holding her in place. "Who's next in line to take the case to trial if you're not able to do it?"

"That choice isn't up to me." She'd worked with only a handful of the other deputies over the years within the county's boundaries, but none of them fit the profile of the man on the bridge. The DA had handpicked her to prosecute this case because of her track record. Ninety-five percent prosecution rate, the highest in the state. The governor had even recommended her to receive the Charles R. English award from the American Bar Association for her distinguished work in the field of criminal justice. "It's at the discretion of the district attorney, Pierce Cook."

Jonah's eyes narrowed on her, hiking her nervous system into overdrive. "This is the biggest domestic terrorism case Oregon has ever seen. Why didn't Cook want to prosecute the case himself?"

"When I met with him for this assignment, he told me he's planning to announce his retirement next month, and he wanted the public and the media to see a strong prosecutor dedicated to bringing this case to the finish line." She'd asked Pierce Cook the same question when he'd brought her into his office the day she'd been assigned this case. She'd met the DA only a few times since she'd come to work for him, but she'd been excited at the prospect of taking on the Rip City Bomber. Now her life—her baby's life—had been put at risk because of it. A knot tightened in her gut. "I haven't talked to anyone in my office since the bombing in the courtroom and you taking me into protective custody. He might've already had me replaced. The justice system doesn't stop just because of attempted murder on the prosecutor."

"The DA hasn't replaced you. Otherwise the bomber wouldn't have reason to finish what he started. I'll have Remington and Cove pay a visit to the DA, see if they can come up with a list of names who match your abductor's profile." Pulling her into his chest, Jonah threaded one hand through her hair as she set her ear over his heart. Right where he needed her. "We're going to get through this."

"How can you be so sure?" Confidence had

come easily for her since she'd pulled herself from that fear-filled life she'd been born into, but now… Madison would have to borrow some of his. She'd have to depend on him to get her through this. The muscles down her back stiffened one by one at the thought, but for as long as she'd been fighting to trust and rely on only herself, the panic never came. Because Jonah would never hurt her. Not intentionally. Without him, she would've died in that courtroom or in her car when she'd tried to leave the scene. She wouldn't have made it to the other side of the bridge. She wouldn't have gotten this far, and the fear she'd hung on to of being in the same situation as her mother—as being trapped by someone who was supposed to care about her—didn't seem to have quite the same meaning anymore. She counted off the steady beats of his heart and closed her eyes. "He could be right outside these walls, waiting for us to make a mistake."

"I don't make mistakes, Maddi," he said. "Especially not when it comes to you."

"Smooth talker." Her mouth tugged into a smile, and suddenly, the past, the divide between them, the fear, none of it seemed as powerful as she'd believed. This moment was for the two of them. Uncertainty and insecurity weren't welcome, and she was able to fully take a breath for the first time she could remember since leaving Los Angeles behind. Because of him. Because of his goodness and dedication to put her first. They'd been friends for years, but in that moment, she could imagine him as more. Not only as the father of her baby but also as a partner.

The low-pitched echo of a ringing phone pulled her back into the moment.

"Don't move a muscle." He spun her around by the hips, keeping one hand on her as he dipped to reach for the phone, and read the screen. The lines between Jonah's eyebrows deepened, and an instant tension filtered through the muscles across his shoulders. "It's Remi."

She couldn't read Jonah's expression. "Why would that matter?"

"I told her I'd catch up with her in the morning. She'd only call me if it was urgent." He slid his thumb across the screen and put the phone at his ear. "Something's wrong."

Worry carved through her the longer he listened. Jonah let his hand slip from her waist, leaving her cold and alone right in front of him. She couldn't make out Remi's words, but the moment he locked his gaze onto hers, she knew. Knew something was wrong. Her stomach soured as all the possibilities lightninged through her mind. Another bombing? An assignment gone wrong for his USMS team? Had somebody been hurt or had her abductor gone after another of the deputy district attorneys? Madison interlaced her fingers beneath her baby bump for assurance, but it never came. An invisible earthquake seemed to streak through her the longer she waited for him to answer.

"When?" Jonah checked his watch. "Thirty minutes ago. Understood. I'll move Madison as fast as I can. I'll be in touch with a new number within the hour."

Move her? Move her where? Why would he need to give his boss a new number? He ended the call, then maneuvered around her for the duffel bag he'd set near the door. "Get your clothes from the bedroom. We're leaving."

"What is it? What happened?" Her heart shot into her throat the longer he refused to look at her. She watched as he double-timed it to the kitchen and threw a few items from the pantry in the bag but didn't answer. He'd transformed into the overprotective, quiet, detail-oriented marshal who'd thrown her into protective custody right after the bombing at the courthouse. Madison reached out. "Jonah, stop. Tell me what is happening."

His pulse beat strong against her fingertips at his wrist, and a hint of the grief he'd hidden behind all these years surfaced. Loosening his grip on the box of granola bars he'd pulled from the pantry, Jonah leveled his gaze on her. "Rosalind Eyler escaped prison thirty minutes ago."

Chapter Twelve

"How…how is that possible?" Madison stumbled away from him, the pink in her cheeks draining from her face, and her grip fell from his wrist.

"We're not sure how yet or why. My team headed to the prison the moment the warden informed the marshals service, and there's an official manhunt in progress for her recapture," he said. "But the evidence says she's been working with the bomber bent on removing you from this case. Rosalind Eyler made some kind of deal with the man who tried to kill you. Stands to reason since he's failed so far, she might be trying to get the job done herself."

"You think she's coming here. For me and the baby." The lack of emotion in her voice grated against his very being. Madison was one of the most hardworking, strategic prosecutors in the state he'd had the pleasure of knowing. He'd watched her win cases with that exact tone of voice interlaced into her arguments, but over these past few days she'd let him see so much more than that. When her internal guards fell away, she was warm, confident and alive. Now the woman standing in front of him had physically, mentally and emotionally prepared herself for the oncoming threat. "I'll get my clothes."

Jonah ignored the constant buzz of warning at the back of his head and encircled his hand around her arm. Pulling her into him, he forced her to look him in the eye. "She'll never lay a hand on you. Understand? I give you my word."

No one was going to take her. No one was going to take their son. No one was going to take his family. Jonah slipped his hands down her arms, waking the nerve endings in his fingers, and a hint of the desire they'd shared notched his body temperature higher.

"I know." The shallow lines around her eyes softened slightly, just for him, as though she'd been reminded of what they'd shared under the sheets in the same moment. "Make sure the next safe house is as perfect as this one, okay?"

"You've got a deal, Counselor." He smiled, releasing her one finger at a time before she turned toward the stairs. "Grab your clothes and meet me back downstairs as soon as you can. We're wheels up in five minutes."

"Aye, aye, Captain." With a half salute, she padded up the stairs and out of sight. Thirty minutes since the prison warden had reported Rosalind Eyler's escape, but that didn't mean that was the exact moment the Rip City Bomber had disappeared. Jonah crossed to the section of wall structuring the stairs and pressed the release for the compartment door he'd had built underneath when he bought the place. A thin, pale wood door matching the rest of the wood grain opened, revealing the wall safe behind it. He pressed his thumb into the reader, and the lock disengaged. Rosalind Eyler was one of the most dangerous criminals he'd encountered throughout the decade he'd been a marshal.

He wasn't leaving anything to chance.

He pulled his backup piece from inside, loaded fresh rounds into the magazine and holstered it under his left pant leg. Closing the safe and the panel door, he hauled the duffel bag filled with their supplies over his uninjured shoulder. They were running out of time. There was no telling what the Rip City Bomber had up her sleeve, but he'd do everything he could to keep Madison out of danger. No matter how long it took. "Maddi, we've got to go."

Her heels clicked on the hardwood as she raced down the stairs with the few items of clothing she'd been able to hold on to. "I didn't want to go on the run in sweatpants."

"Yes, your choice of heels and a skirt was a

much better option." He took her clothes as she hit the bottom step and shoved them inside the bag. By the time Rosalind caught word of this place, he and Madison would be long gone, but his heart jerked at the thought of surrendering the house he'd envisioned protecting his family to a serial bomber. Hesitation gripped him hard.

They could go on the run. They could spend the rest of their lives looking over their shoulders if his team wasn't able to find Rosalind. They could move from safe house to safe house with the possibility of making a mistake thick in their throats.

Or they could give Rosalind and her partner exactly what they'd wanted all along.

He and Madison could be safe. They could move on with their lives. They could raise their son in a stable home with the love he deserved. Together. He could keep her safe. "Rosalind Eyler and the partner she made a deal with want you off the case."

She settled warm caramel-colored eyes on him, and every cell in his body hiked into heated awareness. Three days. That was all it'd taken for him to fall in love with her, to envision her as something more than the mother of his child, more than an assignment, a friend. Madison pointed toward the front. "You're very perceptive. That's why we're leaving, isn't it?"

"What if we didn't have to leave?" he asked.

"What are you talking about? You told Remi you were going to have me moved to another location." Her palms pressed to her baby belly, sleek lines and soft curves tugging at a deeper part of him. He loved her. He was in love with her, and there was nothing that was going to stop him from keeping her safe. Even Madison herself. "Now you want us to stay?"

"I want you to walk away from this alive." Jonah let the duffel bag drop at his feet. He took a step toward her, then another, as pressure built behind his chest. "I want to get to know my son when he's born in a few months, and I want you to recuse yourself as the prosecutor on the Rip City Bomber case."

Ice filled her expression, that automatic guard back in place in an instant, and an immediate wave of cold hit him in the gut. Madison stepped out of his reach, taking the last remnants of heat with her. "You know I can't do that."

"Think about it, Maddi. You weren't pregnant when the DA assigned you to this case. You didn't have a baby to worry about or know how far Rosalind Eyler would go to keep you from prosecuting her." He didn't counter her escape. "She's scared. You're the best prosecutor in the state aside from the DA, and she's desperate to finish what she started, but you're not the only one at risk anymore. If we walk out that door, our son will know nothing more than fear and a life on the run. He deserves better than that. You deserve better than that."

"I'm giving him what he deserves by staying on this case, Jonah." The small muscles in her jaw twitched under pressure. "I'm giving him the future I never had. Prosecuting this case will put me at the front of the line for district attorney once Rosalind Eyler is sentenced, and he'll never have to worry about when his next meal will be, if we're suddenly going to get evicted from our house or if we'll be able to afford shoes for him to go to school. He'll have everything, but only if I can see this through."

"Your life—our son's life—is more important than any job, Madison. Don't you understand that?" He curled his hands into fists as the truth exploded through him. He couldn't lose her, couldn't lose this baby. Not again. He'd tried to ignore it. Chalked it up to the adrenaline over these past few days—to everything they'd been through together—but he couldn't deny it now. "I want us to raise this baby together, here, in this house. I can tell you I've never wanted anything more in my life after what we've been through. I can support you and our son. I can make sure you two have everything you need and more. He won't just not have to worry about where his next meal is coming from, but he'll have two parents to be there to support him as he grows up."

She stepped back as though she'd been hit, the breath rushing out of her. Tears glistened in her eyes as she seemed to regain her balance, but he battled the urge to reach out. He read her answer a split second before the words left her perfectly shaped mouth. "I have to go."

"What?" Shock coursed through him. "Where?"

Diving for the duffel bag he'd discarded on the floor beside his feet, she shouldered their supplies and headed toward the front door. Long hair trailed out from behind her as Madison fled.

"Madison, wait." He threaded his hand between her arm and rib cage in an effort to slow her down, before she made a mistake she couldn't recover from.

"Don't touch me." She turned on him, a hardness in her expression that hadn't been there before, and ripped out of his hold. Her shoulders rose and fell in harsh waves. His fingers stung where her shirt had caused friction, but the oncoming pain of having her walk out that door paralyzed him in place. "I've spent my entire life ensuring I didn't have to depend on anyone, Jonah, but that's exactly what you're asking me to do. All anyone has ever done in my life is betray me, try to control me, and I swore to myself I'd never let someone trap me again." Her knuckles fought to break through the back of her hand as she pointed one long, slim finger at him. "Now you want me to give up on becoming district attorney—of proving I can support this baby without you—so you can have a chance to be a full-time father again."

He swallowed as a rush of grief thickened in his chest.

"I'm sorry you lost Noah all those years ago. I can't imagine how much pain you've had to live with because of that, but I am not helpless." She shook her head. "I am not worthless. I've taken care of myself since the day I turned ten years old, and I don't need a white knight to swoop in and tell me what's best for me and my son. I thought you understood that." The tears fell. "Don't come after us, Jonah. We don't need you."

Her son. Not theirs. Jonah held his ground as she wrenched open the front door and stepped beyond the perimeter of safety. Taking his son with her.

SHE WAS SUPPOSED to be stronger than this.

Madison hauled the bag he'd packed full of food and her clothing toward the SUV and threw it into the passenger seat. Her heels wobbled on the uneven ground, but the rift of hollowness and anger only pushed her harder. She'd gone up against the most terrifying and threatening criminals in the state over the past two years. She'd achieved justice for victims and families, got offenders off the streets, and helped children escape the same fate she'd survived all while holding herself in check every step of the way. But the pressure inside was building to unrecognizable levels.

She collapsed into the driver's seat and gripped the cold leather of the steering wheel, not bothering to check the front door to see if Jonah had followed. She'd trusted him with her body, her entire being. She'd started to believe he would be the last person on earth who'd turn what they had into a domestic cage she wouldn't be able to escape. Just like her mother. Madison pulled down the visor and let the car keys drop into her lap. Swiping at the tears, she twisted the key in the ignition and started the engine.

In seconds, she maneuvered the vehicle down the long dirt road heading back to the main highway. Jonah would have to call someone on his team for a ride. Because she never wanted to see him again. As soon as she reached out to one of her contacts in the Washington State USMS division to have her protection detail transferred to a new marshal, she'd call her lawyer. She'd offered to have her attorney draft a custody and visitation agreement when she'd learned about Jonah's first son's death. She'd wanted to help ease the pain he'd carried all this time, wanted to do something good, but now... Now she understood he'd only used his grief to insert himself into her life. Just as he'd tried to do from the beginning.

Had any of it been real?

The promises? The desire? The way he claimed she made him feel? The tightness in her chest constricted her breathing. Had he cared for her at all or had everything he'd done up until now been only for the sake of their child?

The answer settled at the tip of her tongue. Thick trees and endless miles of dirt stretched out to either side of her as she headed toward the highway. Two and a half hours west before she hit the edge of the city. That was all the time she needed to forget the past three days. Forget the way he'd gone out of his way to protect her, to forget how he'd helped fill the void left behind by her parents' selfishness and neglect. Forget how he'd convinced her to fall in love with him. Leveraging her elbow onto the window ledge of the driver's side door, she rested her temple against her palm. "It wasn't real. None of it could've been real."

The only person she could depend on in this world was herself. She'd learned that as a kid growing up in Los Angeles, learned that as a law student and as a deputy district attorney here in Oregon.

"It's you and me. That's all we need, right?" That was all they needed. That was all she'd ever needed, but the ache around her heart tried to convince her otherwise. Straightening, she slid her hand over her bulging bump. "We're going to make it."

She didn't have any other choice.

Turning east onto Highway 26, she pressed her foot onto the accelerator to get up to speed, but the SUV's engine sputtered. Once. Twice. Black smoke streamed out from the edges of the hood, and the speedometer plummeted toward zero. A strong exhale escaped her control as she pulled the vehicle to the side of the road. Moonlight shone straight overhead as she threw the SUV into Park and pulled at the hood release near her left leg. She looked down at her baby bump. "Do you come programmed with car maintenance know-how? Because apparently your sperm donor does not."

Defeat pulled her deeper into the leather seat. An invisible ache squeezed her chest tighter as she played through the last words she'd spit at Jonah. *We don't need you.* But it hadn't been the truth. Because she'd come to rely on him for more than protection. As more than a rescuer. He'd been safety personified, someone she'd come to trust over her own instincts, a reminder of the good in the world and that she deserved a small piece of it. He'd been…everything.

Right up until he'd broken their unspoken agreement.

She pulled a flashlight from the glove compartment and turned off the car. The edges of the light were sharper than any other she'd used. A tactical flashlight, designed to cause damage if needed and light the way at the same time. Madison waited for a break in traffic before stepping onto the pavement and rounding the hood. She unhitched it and hauled it above her head. Something burnt and sickening dived into her lungs before the smoke cleared. Scanning the caps and knobs—as though she had any idea what the hell made a vehicle function—she focused on one that looked like it might be missing altogether. Heat worked under her blouse from the engine, steam whipping around her as it came into contact with Oregon spring temperatures. The cap was missing, and from the labels on the thick black hose beside the container, it looked like it'd come off the radiator. She peered down into the well but met nothing but blackness. Empty. "You've got to be kidding me."

Another car sped past and the SUV shook slightly. She'd handed over her cell phone to Jonah when he'd taken her into protective custody. She didn't have any way of calling for a tow truck or maintenance, and there were still nearly one hundred miles between her and the city. Technically, there were physically fewer than that between her and Jonah, but she'd walk straight to Portland if that meant never having to face him again. Damn it. She clenched the edge of the SUV's frame. According to him, Deputy Chief Remington Barton required all the marshals on her team to carry emergency supplies and extra fluids for their vehicles. She'd wanted them to be ready for any threat.

Madison wedged herself between the SUV and the highway safety rail to keep from getting hit by an oncoming vehicle and opened the back cargo hatch. Confusion rippled through her. The space was empty. No supplies. No extra ammunition. No gasoline or coolant. That didn't make sense.

Headlights flashed from behind her, and the hairs on the back of her neck stood on end. Jonah wouldn't have taken out his emergency supplies. Not as they were getting ready to move to another safe house. What were the chances of her vehicle running out of coolant in the middle of the night just as she needed to flee the safe house? The supplies were gone. She was stranded. A car door slammed a few feet away, and her heart rocketed into her throat. "Looks like you're having some car troubles. Can I help?"

"No, thank you. I've already called for help." Without being able to see the Good Samaritan's face backlit by blinding headlights, she braved the risk of a vehicle not noticing her on the side of the road and walked toward the driver's side door. She wouldn't be able to drive the SUV as is, but a layer of steel and glass between her and the man behind her was better than nothing.

"Come on now, Madison," he said over the roar

of traffic. "You and I both know you've never been a very good liar. That's what makes you one of the best prosecutors in the state. Your determination to do what's right, even if you're the one who pays the price."

It was him, the man who'd thrown her over the bridge. He'd found her. Fear tensed the muscles down her spine. Hand on the driver's side door, Madison calculated her options for escape. Waving down another car would put innocent lives at risk. Using the SUV as a safe space hadn't worked in her favor at the second bombing scene. Wilderness lined each side of the two-lane highway, but darkness had already fallen. She didn't have time to grab the bag of supplies from the front seat. If she disappeared into the trees, she'd be running blind, running scared and running without hope of the marshals finding her, but it was still her best option.

"There's nowhere for you to run this time, Counselor." He moved in on her, one step at a time. "And no one who's going to save you."

She didn't wait for her abductor to make the first move. Grip tight on the tactical flashlight, she kicked off her heels and dashed straight across the road into westbound traffic. Headlights grew larger a second before a blaring horn screamed in her ears. The pickup truck barely missed hitting her before she fled into the eastbound lane. Loose gravel and uneven pavement cut into her feet as she pumped her legs hard. She cut the power to the flashlight and ran for the guardrail lining the highway, not daring to look back.

Cold steel grazed her thighs as she vaulted over the rail and landed on the other side. Almost there. She just had to reach the trees. He wouldn't be able to find her in the trees. Her heart rate struggled to keep up with her lungs, fingers numb around the flashlight. Dirt bled into thickening weeds ten feet ahead. It was a straight shot. She was almost—

The ground disappeared out from under her.

She lost the flashlight as gravity pulled her down into the steep incline and into a shallow canyon of litter, water and dirt. A scream escaped up her throat before air crushed from her lungs. She hit the bottom on her side, nothing but wide-open sky above her and miles of trees beside her. Salt and copper mixed in a dizzying flood in her mouth. A groan escaped from between her teeth.

Holding on to her belly with one hand, Madison pressed to sit up. Immobilizing pain shot through her wrist and up her arm, and she cried out. Her wrist had possibly broken from the fall. Didn't matter. She had to keep moving. She wouldn't become another victim in this madman's game. She wasn't going to let Rosalind Eyler or her partner win. Not when there was so much to lose.

Gravel crunched under dense footsteps from

behind, and she patted the ground around her to find Jonah's tactical flashlight she'd dropped. "I have to hand it to you, Madison. I didn't think killing you would be this hard. You're a fighter. I appreciate that, but you're only making this harder on yourself."

The footsteps slowed as her fingers felt something heavy and cold. The flashlight. She clicked on the power. Wrapping her fingers around the body, she swung around as hard as she could and met her abductor. Strong fingers locked around her wrist and squeezed. The light from the flashlight cascaded across her attacker's bare face, and recognition flared. No. It wasn't… It wasn't possible. "You?"

"Me." He slammed the edge of the flashlight into her face, and everything went black.

Chapter Thirteen

He shouldn't have let her go.

Rosaline Eyler and her partner were still out there, still a threat, and Madison had escaped down the mountain without any way for him to follow. She might've claimed she didn't need him, but he sure as hell needed her.

Three knocks on the front door reverberated through the house, and Jonah wrenched it open harder than he'd meant.

"You don't call. You don't write. Here I thought we were beginning to become friends after I let your suspect beat the crap out of me." Deputy Marshal Dylan Cove stalked through the front door and took in the raised ceilings. "Why aren't any of my safe houses this nice?"

"Madison left in my SUV twenty minutes ago. We need to find her." Jonah tossed his phone at the marshal with the vehicle's tracking data on the screen as he reached for his Kevlar vest. "According to this, she hasn't moved in minutes, and I'm not giving Rosalind Eyler or her partner a chance to catch up with her. We're running out of time. Where is the rest of the team?"

"Remi is running point on the manhunt for the Rip City Bomber with Reed, Foster and that FBI guy you don't seem to like. Special Agent Jackson." Cove studied the date on the phone. "You get me. You should feel honored."

"Let's go. You drive." Jonah strapped into his vest and holstered his sidearm. In less than thirty seconds, they left the cabin behind and were headed down the mountain. Every cell in his body raced with anxiety. "Where are we at with the list of prosecutors in line to take over the Rip City Bomber case if Madison Gray is unable to perform her duties?"

Cove nodded toward the middle console. "The list is in the file. I took the liberty of pulling phone records, financials and background checks for the top three candidates I got from the district attorney, but I'm not sure what you're hoping to find. All three names came back clean. No visible connection to Rosalind Eyler, no access to the Rip City Bomber case and no evidence any of them has purchased the components to make a homemade bomb in the last twelve months."

Damn it. Their bomber wasn't going to make this easy for them, was he? Jonah skimmed through the file. Two male candidates, one female. He could rule out the female due to evidence and the altercation on the bridge, leaving two males. Cove was right. Background checks, financials, phone records. None of it led to motive for someone inside the district attorney's office, which left Jonah's original suspect, Special Agent Collin Jackson. He scanned through the next section of documents. "You included the statements Reed took from the officers assigned perimeter duty at the second bombing scene."

The bomber had gotten onto and off the scene without the Portland Police Bureau noticing. Or the bastard had presumed clearance to be there. Jonah read through the account of one of the officers assigned to watch the crime scene perimeter on the east end of the street, where forensics had narrowed down the exact spot Madison had been taken. The SUV bounced along the unpaved dirt road as they headed toward the highway, but that didn't stop Jonah from highlighting a single name as the rest of the text bled away. He turned the statement toward Cove. "This officer states he let only one person under the tape while he was on duty that day, but never saw the man leave. Want to guess who?"

Cove focused on the name Jonah underscored with his finger. "You've got to be kidding me."

"He had the means and the opportunity. I

should've seen it before now. I should've known."
Jonah pulled his phone from his pocket and dialed
the deputy chief. The bomber hadn't been law enforcement at all, but the SOB might as well have
been considering his access to the investigation
and the Rip City Bomber case. Hell, how had he
missed it? And how the hell had the bastard been
able to keep tabs on Madison? The line connected,
and he put the call on speaker. "Remi, I need everything you have on Pierce Cook. Now."

"The district attorney?" Surprise laced her
question, but the remoteness of her voice said
she'd put him on speaker, presumably to keep her
hands free to get him what he'd asked for. "I need
you to be one hundred and ten percent sure about
this, Watson. The second I put in this request, I'm
going to have the governor on my back asking why
I pulled background on the most popular elected
official in the state."

He had to be sure. The Oregon USMS division
wasn't the only one who'd suffer if he made a mistake. Madison would lose her job completely, lose
everything she'd ever worked for. He'd already
blown his chance of turning what they had into
something more, of them raising their son together.
He couldn't ruin this for her, too.

Jonah strengthened his hand around the phone.
"Madison told me Pierce Cook is scheduled to announce his retirement in the next month, that he

put her on the Rip City Bomber case because he wanted a strong prosecutor to see the case through to the end. But a case like this would put him down in the history books for life. What if assigning her this case hadn't been his choice? His term is coming to an end. Madison's been recognized by the governor for her work. It'd be easy to confirm the governor is the one who assigned Madison the case and not the district attorney as we believed. He could've just been responsible for giving her the assignment."

"I think you might be right," Remi said. "Not only does he have the experience with explosives during his two tours with the army, but I logged into Portland Police Bureau's database to run a background check. He requested their IT department run GPS on Madison Gray's cell phone three days ago. Just minutes after the bombing at the courthouse."

"I took her phone after she was cleared by the EMTs, but he could've been trying to get a hold of her after he caught wind of what happened. We need something more. Something solid." He turned to Cove as they pulled onto Highway 26. "GPS says my SUV hasn't moved in ten minutes about a mile ahead. Watch out for her."

"Watson, Madison's GPS location wasn't the only data requested that day." Her voice grew distant. "The DA had them track yours, too."

"Which means Pierce Cook knew where his target was all along. He used me to track her. All he had to do was get her alone." His voice sounded distant, even to himself, as Jonah caught sight of red reflective taillights off to the side of the road ahead. A knot of dread pooled at the base of his spine as Cove signaled to pull behind the dark SUV. GPS confirmed his vehicle hadn't moved, and from a cursory inspection, there wasn't any movement inside. "She's not here." Blood drained from his face and upper body, suctioning him to the seat. He clutched his phone too tight. "He was waiting for her, watching her. I let her walk out that door and right into the bastard's hands."

Cove didn't respond as he shoved the vehicle in Park and shouldered out of the vehicle.

"Reed and Foster are wrapped up in the manhunt for Rosalind Eyler," Remi said. "Tech guys are working to find a location on Pierce Cook's phone now. I'll send you the coordinates as soon as they get a clear signal and join you as soon as I can. If he's taken her, it won't take us long to catch up. If not, we'll find out what he was doing trying to locate a federal marshal and his witness without going through the proper channels. Either way, we're going to find her, Jonah. This is what we do."

She ended the call as he hit the pavement and unholstered his weapon. With a nod, he signaled for Cove to move in, battle-ready tension pulling at the muscles in his back. Approaching the SUV from either side, he and the other marshal inspected the open hatch, noting the missing supplies he always kept on hand, and the back seat. He wrenched the passenger side door open and froze. Empty aside from the keys still in the ignition. She wouldn't have walked away. Pierce Cook had shattered a window to get to Madison at the second scene, but as far as he could tell, there hadn't been a struggle here. She'd vanished. No phone, no emergency supplies, no sign of her. What the hell had happened here? "Clear."

"Jonah," Cove said.

He rounded the front of the vehicle where the former private investigator stood staring down at the engine, the hood propped open above him.

"Radiator's completely dry." Cove pointed to the section clearly missing a cap. "Every vehicle the USMS owns is serviced before we check them out, no exceptions, but there are a few drops of fluid on the asphalt by my feet. If I had to guess, someone took a screwdriver to the well and drained it dry."

"Not someone. Pierce Cook." Jonah had no doubts now. The district attorney had tried to kill his successor—twice—and had murdered a defense attorney in the process. Now Cook would spend his retirement behind bars. Jonah would make sure of it. He shifted around to the driver's side of the SUV, headlights of their vehicle highlighting a pristine pair of tan heels, and his world shattered. "I've got her shoes here."

Cove crossed the white line indicating the highway shoulder. "So the car overheats, and she has to pull over. She gets out, pops the hood. There's probably smoke, but your lady is intelligent. She realizes the radiator well is empty, and she needs to refill it if she's going to make it back to the city."

"She knows marshals are required to carry emergency fluids for their vehicles, but when she opens the back hatch, she discovers the supplies are missing." Jonah could see the story playing out in his mind, and he locked his hand on the frame of the SUV. She was out here somewhere. Afraid. Alone. He'd been an idiot asking her to resign from the Rip City Bomber case, asking her to give up her one ounce of security in a life filled with uncertainty and fear. As if he'd known what she'd survived as a kid and decided right then and there none of it mattered. She'd believed in him, and he'd failed her. She was a strong, independent woman who'd taken on the deadliest offenders for a single chance to bring justice to the families that depended on her, and he loved her for it. Demanding Madison let go of her dream to become district attorney—to support their son on her own—had been like demanding he simply forget Noah. He'd regret that last conversation between them for the rest of his life. "That's when he drives up behind her. She doesn't have a phone or a weapon. So she kicks off her shoes—"

"To run." Cove stared across the highway, toward the trees on the other side. "Question is, did she run fast enough?"

HER FEET WERE COLD against the cement.

She couldn't take a full breath, as though something heavy was squeezing the air from her lungs. Madison dragged her chin away from her chest, head pounding. Small kicks protested against the heaviness around her belly. The baby didn't like something invading his space, least of all her rib cage. The edges of her vision cleared in small increments as her eyes adjusted to a single bare bulb above her. Her shoulder sockets ached, but she couldn't pull her hands around to her front. She'd been bound by the wrists. Pressing her toes into the floor, she tipped the chair on its hind legs, but her ankles wouldn't move. Her abductor had zip-tied her feet to the frame. Without something to cut through the plastic, she was trapped.

"I was starting to think I might've hit you so hard you were going to miss out on all the fun." From the corner of the room, the outline of the man who'd attacked her nearly bled into the background. His shadow separated from the wall as he took a step toward her into the radius of light. No mask. Nothing to hide now.

Her boss, District Attorney Pierce Cook, settled hard light green eyes on her, and her heart threatened to beat straight out of her chest. He ran one hand through dark brown hair peppered with gray. Thick forehead wrinkles deepened as he studied her, a handsome face she'd come to trust over the years. He'd once stood as the face of justice for the city. Now he'd become one of its worst.

Pierce reached past her right ear and wrapped his hand around the top rail of the chair. He leaned in, too close. "Do you know how many cases I've prosecuted for this city, Madison? How many criminals I've put away over the years? How many neighborhoods I made safe by committing my life to this work? I built a legacy here. Right up until the governor forced my resignation, until he forced me to put you on the Rip City Bomber case. He took that from me, but now I can make it right."

That was why he was doing this? Why he'd killed nine innocent people, including Harvey Braddock, and tried to throw her off a bridge? Anger stirred in her gut as the pieces fell into place. The bombing, destroying evidence of murder at Harvey Braddock's home, how the bomber had seemed to stay one step ahead of US marshals and police. It was all to serve his ego. "Of all the people I believed in, Pierce, you were the beacon I looked up to my entire career. You were the reason I applied for a job in the district attorney's office. You were legendary. There wasn't a single case you couldn't take on and win, and I imagined myself following in your footsteps. I'm the prosecutor I am because of you." She tried to breathe through the weight still limiting her lung capacity, but it took effort. Twisting her wrists inside the zip tie, Madison tried to keep her expression neutral as the plastic cut into her skin. "But now you're no better than the people we prosecute. Murderers, drug dealers, rapists. It doesn't matter how many cases you've won or how many criminals you've kept off the streets. All anyone is going to remember you for is this."

A close-lipped smile slithered across his weathered face. "No, Madison. They won't. Because in about twenty-five minutes, you won't be alive to tell them anything other than the story I've come up with to explain everything that's happened."

Twenty-five minutes? Why—

The bulk on her chest registered again, and for the first time since waking, she realized why it'd become so hard to breathe. The Kevlar vest he'd strapped her into had been tightened enough to conceal the bright red digits counting down across her chest. Precious oxygen lodged in her throat. He'd turned her into a bomb.

"You see, everything I've done, every bomb I detonated, every loose end I tied up, none of it can be connected back to me," he said.

Realization struck.

"You took credit for those bombings in the Rip City Bomber's name. To frame Rosalind Eyler." She tried to swallow. "You're the partner she made her behind-the-scenes deal with before the first attack. She gave you the list and measurements of the components she used in her devices in exchange for what? Had to be something important to Rosalind to give up that kind of information. Reduced sentencing, a chance to finish the work she started with her coworkers? She wouldn't tell us. I think she was trying to protect her partner. Stands to reason, as her partner, you couldn't do that unless you were the one behind the prosecution's table to offer the deal, and that meant you had to get rid of me. You get to step back into the limelight and leave behind the legacy you've always wanted, and Rosalind gets a deal. Everyone walks away happy."

"Well, not everyone." Pierce shook his head. Straightening, he stepped back a few feet as his voice dipped with frustration. "If that damn marshal hadn't managed to catch up with us at the falls, we would've been able to put this all behind us sooner." He drove his hands into his slacks pockets. "Of course, asking you to step down from the case wasn't an option. We've only met a few times, but I've watched your work all these years. I see that drive I have to rise to the top in you.

I know there's nothing I could've said or done to make you recuse yourself from the Rip City Bomber trial, but I couldn't let you take this from me."

The puzzle was starting to make sense as she read between the lines of the district attorney's phrasing, but there was a hole in this fantasy. "There's one problem with your plan, Pierce. You failed to consider the fact Rosalind Eyler killed thirty-two people for taking credit for her academic work, and she knows what you've been doing in her name. How do you think she's going to react when she catches up with you?"

A sincere moment of fear turned Pierce's eyes down at the corners. So subtle she might not have noticed if she hadn't been looking straight at him. "If Rosalind's as smart as all those degrees and IQ tests claim, she'll do exactly as I tell her and be grateful her last moments on this earth will be behind bars and not with a needle in her arm."

"Breaking her out of prison wasn't part of the plan." She had to keep him talking, keep him distracted. Madison pressed her wrists together inside the restraints and put everything she had into creating enough pressure to snap the zip tie. The plastic wouldn't budge. "What about Harvey Braddock? You obviously used his garage to build your devices, but was his murder always part of this plan?"

"Harvey had his uses. If you'd become district attorney, you would've learned there are some things—some people—worth sacrificing in order to win." Pierce crossed to the other side of the room. Shadows clung to the area outside the spread of light around her, but the reflection of the bulb off the rolltop door said this was most likely some kind of storage room. The district attorney rooted through objects spread across a folding table along one wall. He picked one up, studied it, discarded it. Then another as though trying to choose the perfect torture device to threaten her with. "Harvey knew about the deal between me and Rosalind Eyler. He was on board with it. Right up until he learned you were the target. The idiot threatened to go to the marshals, said he didn't want any part of having you killed in order to get his client the best deal." Pierce turned back toward her, and the hairs on the back of her neck stood on end. "He wanted to take his chances with the jury, but I couldn't have that."

The countdown hadn't stopped, red lights demanding her attention from the dark space between her chest and the Kevlar vest. "You stole the thermite to draw Marshal Watson out into the open and kill Harvey all at the same time. Two birds, one stone. You figured the marshal who'd taken me into protective custody would be forced to leave me with someone else while he was on that scene."

And it'd worked. Pierce had gotten exactly what he'd wanted that day, and the only reason she was still breathing was because of Jonah. Because of how far he'd gone to make sure she walked away from this mind game alive.

"I saw the way you two are around each other. The late nights, the early mornings. I found those homemade crosswords you'd make him to keep him busy while you worked. I had to know who'd get in my way, so I looked into him, too. Luring him into the field with an explosive only he had experience with was the only way I was going to get him away from you, and that gave me the perfect opportunity." Pierce leaned against the table, and for the first time, she recognized the dusty objects on the surface.

Phones, duct tape, box cutter, glass vials with residue clinging to the sides. Pieces that, in the right order, could be constructed into a bomb, but this wasn't Pierce's original laboratory. He'd destroyed that with evidence of Harvey Braddock's murder in the garage. The courthouse bomb and the device left undetonated inside Harvey Braddock's home had been built with the ammonium nitrate from ice packs. Here, it looked as though the bomber had made his own, as Rosalind had revealed that day at the prison. The thickness of dust coating the table, in the air, suggested a much older lab. Could this storage container belong to the Rip City Bomber? Police hadn't ever been able to locate it, but Pierce obviously had. Was this where he'd meant for investigators—for Jonah— to find her body in order to strengthen his plan to frame Rosalind Eyler? As far as she knew, Jonah hadn't even realized she was in danger or that she'd been taken.

"I know Marshal Watson is the father of your baby, Madison. I know how far he'll go out of his way to protect the people he cares about, especially another child after everything he went through losing his first." He pushed off from the table with the roll of duct tape and tore a piece free. Slapping it against her mouth, he ensured no one would hear her. Pierce reached high above her head—to the string beside the bare bulb—and tugged it.

Darkness consumed the space and threw her into a frantic emptiness that reminded her of all those times she'd hidden in strangers' car trunks to get away from her father. Panic sent numbness down her fingers.

Footsteps clued her in to Pierce's movement as he crossed to the rolltop door and hauled it above his head. Dim light flooded through the corridor from the other side, giving her a glimpse of row after row of storage units. The district attorney paused, his expression as dark as the shadows closing in around her. "Only he isn't coming to save you this time. No one is."

He stepped back and started to pull the door down.

"No!" Madison screamed as loud as the tape would let her, but it wasn't enough. She tried to kick out. He couldn't leave her here. "No!"

The sound of a padlock clicked into place.

Chapter Fourteen

"I had a ping from Pierce Cook's phone two minutes ago on the east side of the city, but I lost it a
second later. He must've shut the phone off as soon
as he arrived, or destroyed it." Static cut through
Remi's voice as Jonah and Cove exceeded the highway's speed limits. Jagged rocks and boulders bled
into uniform darkness before Portland came into
view. "Corner of Stark Street and Twenty-Second
Avenue. I'm on my way with backup."

"We're five minutes out, Chief." Cove maneuvered the SUV around a slower vehicle and pushed
the engine harder.

"Cove's and my priority needs to be recovering
Madison. Taking Pierce Cook down will have to
be your job. Just make sure it hurts when you put
the cuffs on him." Jonah ended the call and scram-
bled to remember what was in the area of where
Cook's phone had pinged off the towers. Car parts
store, apartment buildings, martial arts studio, car

rental. None of those was conducive to holding a hostage…or getting rid of a body. The district attorney would need a private location. Somewhere with a reduced traffic of people in the middle of the night. Somewhere nobody might hear Madison scream. "There's a large storage unit facility on the southeast corner of that intersection."

"Perfect location to make sure your victim can't escape if locked inside." Dylan Cove didn't elaborate. The former private investigator didn't have to. "Those storage places have hundreds of units, though, and we don't have time to search every single one of them. We're going to have to narrow this down."

The marshal was right. Every second Madison was missing was another second Pierce Cook had to kill her. They couldn't waste their time focusing on the wrong areas, and time was already running out. They maneuvered into the turnout leading to the storage facility's parking lot, met by a large gate. Cove lowered the window and flashed his badge to the security officer inside the booth positioned outside the premises. "US Marshals. We have reason to believe a victim has been abducted and hidden inside one of these units. We need to search the property." Dylan Cove showed a photo of their perp to the attendant. "Have you seen this guy come through here tonight?"

"Yeah, man. He came through about thirty

minutes ago. In a hurry. Haven't seen him leave, though. He's dangerous?" The security attendant's gaze widened, and he hit the button to release the gate. "I need to call my boss."

Cove shot the SUV through the partially open gate, then parked off to one side.

Jonah shoved out of the vehicle, and they both rounded to the rear, gearing up. Jonah pushed through the pain in his shoulder and side and reached for the shotgun case. He loaded three rounds into the stock and added three more to his vest for easy access. His pistol was enough to take down any threat, but he couldn't waste time trying to get inside one of these storage units by hand. The shotgun would do the job. He closed the space between him and the security officer. "Which unit does that man own?"

"I…I have no idea." The attendant slid the phone down his cheek, then pointed off to their right. "But he drove that way."

Hell. Jonah studied the long row of structure after structure. Twenty, thirty, forty units, all barely lit with flickering and worn-out lighting on the outside. It would take time to search them all. Time Madison didn't have. Hauling the stock of the shotgun against his shoulder, he angled the barrel toward the pavement and took up position along the right side of the first row. "You take the left. Open any one of these units if you feel you have cause. Keep your ears open and your eyes peeled for anything out of the ordinary. According to the attendant, Pierce is still here."

Shadows jumped from unit to unit as Jonah kept himself pressed against the wall, stopping at each unit only for a moment before moving on to the next. No cries for help. No sign of her or the bastard who'd taken her. Doubt coiled low in his gut. The cell towers had pinged Pierce Cook's location near this storage facility. Had he been wrong in assuming this was where the district attorney had taken his prey?

A scrape of metal echoed off the steel rolltop doors and both Cove and Jonah slowed as they neared the end of the row. With a glance at the former private investigator, he signaled for Cove to use caution with two fingers. Jonah was in the dark from this side of the alley. No sight lines, but also perfectly positioned to move on the target quickly.

Cove pressed his back flat against the unit behind him and leaned his head to the left to survey the source of the noise. Straightening, he nodded, then crossed the narrow alleyway to join Jonah on the other side. "Single suspect, looks like Cook, loading boxes into the back of a moving truck. No sign of Madison with him."

"She has to be in one of the units in the next row." Only problem, which one? Moving trucks didn't exactly fit in these narrow alleys, forcing the district attorney to park at the end of the row, which meant Pierce Cook had most likely used a dolly system to get from his unit to the truck. "I don't care what you have to do to bring him down, but I want him alive. He's the only one who can tell us which unit she's in. Understand?"

"Copy." Deputy Marshal Dylan Cove loaded a round into his sidearm and nodded. "Ready when you are."

"Move." Jonah rounded the corner, shotgun raised, and caught sight of their suspect loading the last of whatever he'd come for into the back of the truck. "District Attorney Pierce Cook, you're under arrest. Turn around, interlace your hands behind your head and get down on your knees. Now."

The man at the rear of the truck straightened slowly, his back to both marshals. Dark hair skimmed along the back of the suspect's sweater collar before he turned to face them. Pierce Cook leveled light-colored eyes on them. Confirmation. They had him. "Marshal Watson, I take it this isn't a social call. Now, just so I get this right when I call the governor in the morning to have your badge, exactly what crime are you accusing me of?"

"Murder of nine people, including Harvey Braddock, kidnapping of Madison Gray, attempted murder of a deputy district attorney, three counts of use of explosives in a public area." Jonah took one step, then another. "Want me to keep going? I'm sure the prosecutor at your trial will have a lot more."

"Trial? I'm not going to trial, Marshal. You can arrest me, but I guarantee I won't spend more than an hour behind bars. I haven't done anything wrong." Pierce squared off as though ready for a fight. "I was sorry to hear about what happened to Madison. Almost killed in that courthouse bombing, then abducted by a masked man from Harvey Braddock's home and nearly thrown over a bridge. I can't imagine how awful you must feel considering you were the one who was supposed to protect her and her baby, but the fact of the matter is neither you nor the USMS have evidence connecting me to any of what you just said."

"Where is she?" Jonah strengthened his grip on the shotgun, his instincts focused on neutralizing the threat to his family. To his future.

"I don't know what you're talking about, but I have a feeling you might be too late." The district attorney's mouth smoothed into a twisted smile under a thick beard as he turned back to continue loading the equipment into the truck.

Jonah stepped into the DA's personal space and pressed the shotgun into Pierce's spine. "I said get on your knees and interlace your hands behind your head."

"Are you going to shoot me if I don't comply, Marshal Watson? You want to, don't you? You want to save the damsel in distress from the big, bad bomber, but like I said—you're too late." Faster than Jonah expected, Pierce Cook spun, slamming his palm against the shotgun to divert the barrel down and to the right. A hard kick from the district attorney landed square in Jonah's gut, and he fell back into the marshal behind him.

Both men went down as Pierce Cook disappeared behind the moving truck.

"Stay on him!" Jonah shoved to his feet. Pumping his legs as fast as he could, he maneuvered around the truck and chased after the fleeing suspect already two rows ahead of him. Heavy breathing and pounding footsteps echoed from behind as he and Cove closed in on their suspect. Pierce wasn't getting away. That wasn't how this was going to end. He was going to find Madison alive. He was going to tell her how much of a mistake he'd made. He was going to spend the rest of his life proving he could make her and their son happy without forcing her to give up her independence. "Pierce!"

Sirens and screeching tires ahead redirected the DA down another row of units.

Jonah pointed to the row next to him. "Cut him off!"

Cove branched off to the right to get to Pierce from the other side.

Jonah's heart pounded hard in his chest, his legs going numb from the slap of his boots against pavement. He turned down the row where Pierce had disappeared, weapon drawn, and halted short.

The district attorney stood in the middle of the alley, a large serrated blade pressed to his throat. Pierce Cook's shoulders rose and fell in shallow waves, but it was the woman standing behind him Jonah couldn't take his eyes off of. "Marshal, please. Help me."

Rosalind Eyler slid the tip of her nose up the length of the district attorney's neck as though savoring every moment of fear she could wring out of the man under her knife. "Did you really think you could use my blueprints, my name, for your dirty work and not suffer the same as all the rest of them, Pierce? I've known men like you my entire life. I've killed men like you. You were never going to hold up your end of the deal, and I won't let you take advantage of one more woman."

"Rosalind, put the knife down." Jonah took aim, but even from a closer position, he still risked hitting the district attorney instead of her. He needed Cook alive to tell them where he'd stashed Madison. There was no other option. "He'll spend the rest of his life in prison for what he's done. That's punishment enough. Put down the knife, or I will pull this trigger."

"I believe you." Rosalind settled bright green

eyes on him, her smile wider than he'd ever seen it before, then slid the knife across Pierce Cook's throat. The DA collapsed out of her grip and slumped to the pavement. "Oops."

"No!" Jonah kept his gun on her as he ran toward Pierce.

A gunshot tore through Rosalind's shoulder from behind, and she fell forward with the momentum. Dylan Cove jogged into view, gun trained on the fugitive, and kicked the blade the Rip City Bomber had used out of her reach.

Jonah holstered his weapon and pressed the heel of his palms against the DA's throat. Blood trickled up through his fingers as he applied pressure, but the man's eyes remained distant and unmoving. "Stay with me, Pierce. Tell me where she is, damn it. Tell me!"

MADISON FLINCHED AT the sound of the single gunshot.

She couldn't hear anything, couldn't see anything. Was someone out there? Was someone looking for her?

Jonah. His name pierced through the panic she'd given in to for the last few minutes. She forced herself to take a deep breath to get her heart rate under control. Alone, in the dark, she pulled at her bound wrists and ankles for the hundredth time, but Pierce had done too good of a job ensuring she couldn't escape. Five minutes. The countdown ticked off second by second, and there was nothing she could do to stop it. Nothing she could do to save herself or her baby. Tape sucked the moisture from her mouth.

Screaming wouldn't do any good. She'd have to find another way to get someone's attention. She wasn't going to die here. She wasn't going to let the last conversation between her and Jonah stand. He'd asked her to let go of the future she'd worked her entire life to build—to trust him with every ounce of her being that he wouldn't hurt her—and she'd said no. But now she understood the role fear had played in her life leading her to this exact moment. Fear of relying on someone who'd end up hurting her, fear of being that small, helpless girl she'd left behind. Fear of being unloved and used. Every decision she'd made over the course of her life had been out of fear.

Until Jonah. Where the past had filled her with hollowness and isolation all these years, he'd brought light, warmth, commitment. She'd learned to expect the worst of the people who were supposed to care about her, but the emotional, physical and mental neglect had only prepared her to view everyone the same, to distance herself from getting too close. And when he'd asked her to recuse herself from the case, he'd offered nothing but respect, support and space, and it'd scared her. She hadn't been able to see the ulterior motive—still didn't—but now she understood. Jonah didn't have one. He never had.

And she was tired of letting fear build her future.

Ankles zip-tied to the frame of the chair, Madison pressed her toes into the floor and tipped forward. Getting oxygen was still hard, her lungs working overtime from the weight of the vest and the tape over her mouth, but she'd do whatever it took to get out of there. The two back legs lifted off the cement. She tensed against the chair. She could do this. She had to do this. Slowly, one inch at a time, she angled her toes out, then in, and crossed the storage unit toward the table, the rest of her body following.

Four minutes.

Only the sound of her pounding pulse filled her ears. No more gunshots. No sounds of footsteps telling her someone was coming to save her. She had to save herself. An overly loud thump registered as the back of the chair hit the edge of the table, and she set the chair back on all four feet. She'd made it across the unit, but without something to cut through the zip ties, she'd still be here when the clock ran out. Her arms ached from the position she'd been tied in, but it wouldn't be enough to stop her now. What was on the table? Duct tape. Cell phones.

She'd gotten only a glimpse of the rest before

Pierce had shut her inside the darkness. Rosalind Eyler and the district attorney both would've needed tools to assemble their devices. Box cutters. She'd noticed the tool before Pierce had locked her inside. That would work, but her hands were still tied. She didn't have time to try to cut through the zip ties or to try to get one of the cell phones to work. Pressure built in her chest as she read the countdown.

Three minutes.

She'd wasted too much time.

"Come on." Both words disappeared behind the tape secured across her mouth. She needed someone to know where she was. Noise. She needed to find something to make noise and pray it was loud enough to draw their attention.

The unit's walls were built of cinder block, but the rolltop door was presumably steel. Steel could be loud when hit with something hard, but to get to the door she'd have to cross the unit again. She rocked forward onto her toes but miscalculated the angle. Falling forward, Madison slammed onto her right arm with the chair on top of her. Her scream lodged in her mouth as the air crushed from her lungs. Her broken wrist from falling down the incline on the highway burned. She couldn't see, couldn't breathe, and the panic flared. Rawness tore along her throat as sobs took control. Trying to rip her other arm free of the tie, she rocked back and forth against the floor. The chair knocked against the cinder blocks.

She stilled. The sound could be enough to draw whoever'd shot that gun.

Two minutes.

Madison bit back the pain in her arm pinned between the chair and the cement and rocked the frame into the cinder blocks. Once. Twice. She closed her eyes, losing count, as tears streaked across her face. She wouldn't look at the count-down again. Couldn't let that be her last memory. She'd think about Jonah instead, about their son, their future. She'd think about how happy they would've been if she hadn't been so afraid of let-ting go of all the hurt and pain. The tears dried.

Distorted voices reached through the darkness. Then again.

Opening her eyes, Madison moaned through the tape. She rocked the chair back into the wall harder, accompanied by her pathetic attempt to shout for help. Metal protested in her ears, then a loud bang right before the rolltop door screamed along the track. Several holes had been punctured through the steel. Fresh air rushed into the unit as two outlines took stock of what was inside.

She tried to crane her head up, but managed only to strain the muscles in the back of her neck. Another shout for help died at her lips.

"Maddi!" The largest of the two outlines collapsed at her side and made quick work of the zip ties. Her uninjured hand immediately went to pull the tape from her mouth as Jonah cut through the ties at her ankles, and a surge of warning shot through her. "I've got you. I've got you."

She sucked in as much air as she could. "Bomb… Vest. Get out."

"I'm not going anywhere without you, damn it. Not again." Cutting her loose from the chair, Jonah pulled her into a sitting position against the wall, his cinnamon-spiced aftershave diving deep into her lungs. He'd come for her. Even after she'd told him she didn't need him, he'd come for her. "Somebody get that light on. I need to be able to see what I'm doing so I don't blow us all to hell."

The light burst to life overhead, and Madison closed her eyes against the brightness. Someone else was in the unit. A woman. His deputy chief?

The sound of Velcro tearing filled the space as Jonah exposed the device Pierce had strapped to her chest. "Pierce can't hurt you anymore. He can't hurt anyone anymore. Okay? He's gone."

Pierce was dead?

One minute.

Her pulse rocketed into dangerous territory. They didn't have enough time. As much as she hated the idea of the district attorney finishing what he'd started, Madison couldn't be responsible for bringing two US marshals down with her. "Jonah, you have to go."

"Don't move." He worked fast, examining each wire running from the cell phone duct-taped to the small plastic container near her chest, then moved on to the next. This was what he'd been trained for. This was what he did best, but not even the most experienced bomb technicians were fireproof. "The bastard added a bunch of dead wires to confuse anyone who might've found you in time."

"I'll order everyone back." Remi's voice brought Madison's attention up to the deputy chief angled over Jonah's shoulder before the marshal called to the growing scene outside the door. "Active explosive! I need everyone to evacuate behind the perimeter. Now!"

"I can't cut you out," Jonah said. "He's got the wires running down through the vest."

"Jonah, you're running out of time." She couldn't be the reason he died.

"No, I'm not going to lose you. You're not dying in here today. Understand?" He locked mesmerizing blue eyes on her, and the entire world fizzled into nothingness. In that moment, there was only the two of them. That was all they needed. Nothing else mattered. He pinched what looked like a blue wire between his index finger and thumb. "Do you trust me?"

No hesitation this time. No fear. "I've always trusted you. I love you."

"I love you, too." Jonah pulled the wire free from the device. The countdown on the LED screen stopped for a moment, then flickered before speeding up to twenty seconds remaining. He flipped open the blade he must've used to cut through her zip ties and sliced the Kevlar vest holding the device down the side. He peeled her out and helped her haul the heavy bulk over her head, as she'd done for him back in the ambulance after the courthouse explosion.

Terror stirred in her gut. "What—"

"There was no way to disarm it without triggering the final countdown." He tossed the vest toward the back of the room, latched onto her hand with his and pulled her out of the storage unit. Turning back briefly, he pulled the rolltop door shut. A soft beeping reached under the space between the door and the cement as they ran for safety. He waved toward the marshals standing near the moving truck Pierce Cook had used to abduct her from the highway. "Get back!"

An ear-deafening explosion thundered through the alleyway from behind.

Heat seared across her skin as tendrils of flames and hot air raced ahead of her and Jonah. He wrapped his arms around her, protecting her from the sear of the blast. She ducked her head between her hands as chunks of metal and stone rained down on top of them. Debris bounced against asphalt under their feet. He kept her moving ahead of him. Smoke enveloped them in a thick layer of blackness, but he wouldn't let her stop. Adrenaline drained from her veins as quickly as it'd set in and made every step heavier than the last.

Then the smoke cleared.

Chapter Fifteen

Hell, he'd never hurt like this. Inside, outside and everything in between, but it was nothing compared to the relief making its way through him. Jonah tried to wipe the dried blood off his hands, but ended up only making the mess worse. He tossed the damp rag one of the EMTs had given him into the back of the ambulance and stared out over the scene.

Portland police had already created a two-row perimeter within the storage facility's gates. The owner had been reached and brought down to assess which units belonged to which tenants. With as much damage as the property had suffered because of a federal investigation, tenants would most likely be reimbursed for the whole thing. Special Agent Collin Jackson was already searching the recently extinguished remains of Pierce Cook's storage unit for evidence while firefighters checked the rest of the area for hot spots. The unknown bomb tech hadn't been involved in the plot on Madison's life after all, but Jonah wouldn't ignore the suspicion still nagging him at the back of his mind. Not a single teammate in his former unit back at Quantico had heard of the agent. Could be Agent Jackson was too new to the field, could be something else. Right now, Jonah had more important priorities on his mind. His deputy chief gave orders from under a temporary command tent with Dylan Cove at her side, both Marshals Reed and Foster ready for their next move.

Morning broke over the horizon to the east, casting warm golden light across the pavement, and for the first time in four days, he was able to breathe. It was over. Madison and the baby were safe, and the SOB behind the latest bombings would soon be under six feet of dirt. What that meant for him and the mother of his unborn child, Jonah didn't know. He'd almost lost her for good this time, but he'd managed to stay under complete control when faced with the device strapped to her chest. A straight-up miracle if he'd ever seen one.

His entire life he'd wanted nothing more than to have what his parents had given him inside their small family. Love, devotion, support. He'd had that with Noah for the short weeks after his son had been born. He'd been happy rocking his newborn to sleep for hours and still couldn't get enough when he'd set Noah in his crib. He'd been whole. Up until his mother had called with the news his child had passed away in his sleep, and in a few short months, he'd be faced with that possibility again. Only this time, there was a chance he wouldn't have to shoulder it alone.

Madison smoothed her hands over her growing belly as she gave her statement to one of the uniformed officers off to his right. Long dark hair constructed a waterfall down her back, concealing her face as she laid out the details of what'd happened between her and the district attorney. She and Jonah had managed to escape the blast with nothing more than aches, a few scratches and bruises. He'd been seconds away from moving on to the next row of units when he'd heard the soft pounding behind one of the rolltop doors, and his instincts had told him everything he'd needed to know. He'd found her. Despite the fact she'd been zip-tied to a chair and strapped with a homemade bomb vest, right then Jonah had never seen a more perfect vision highlighted by the spotlights PPB set up around the scene.

His future.

"You've still got a bit of ash on your face." Remington Barton settled against the bumper of the ambulance and stared out over the scene. Sunlight hit light blue eyes just right, nearly making them colorless. Long sleeves brushed against the backs of her hands as she gripped the vehicle's frame, and Jonah caught a hint of a tattoo against her wrist. He'd never known Remi to wear short sleeves. Never known her to talk about her past. Seemed he wasn't the only one keeping secrets from the team. "Sounds like Madison Gray is still in the running for district attorney with Pierce Cook gone. After everything that's gone down over the past few days and having a front-row seat to how far she'll go to prosecute Rosalind Eyler, she's certainly got my vote."

Jonah couldn't take his eyes off the woman in question. "Mine, too."

"Special Agent Jackson was able to pull a fingerprint from the courthouse bomb after the crime scene techs collected all the evidence. It belonged to Pierce Cook." Remi crossed one ankle over the other. "He used his security clearance to plant the device about a month before the construction was complete. Makes sense, since he and the judge would've been the only two to know which courtroom they'd be prosecuting the Rip City Bomber case in, but we had the bomb squad tear through nearly every inch in the building to make sure. No other devices were recovered."

"He'd been planning on this for a while," Jonah said. "Probably since the day the governor forced Cook to step down from his position and hand the case off to Madison."

"Guess we'll never know. Rosalind Eyler made

sure of that." Remi pushed off from the ambulance and stepped up beside him. Gesturing with her chin toward the patrol car at the end of the row, she watched officers load the Rip City Bomber into the back of the vehicle. "They'll add another nine counts of murder, conspiracy and attempted murder to her charges, but I don't think she regrets any of it."

Compelling green eyes locked on him from across the parking lot as Rosalind Eyler paused. A hint of a smile curved at her mouth. Whatever kind of deal she'd made with Pierce Cook wouldn't hold up in the coming months of trial. She'd have to appeal to Madison, and a knot of uncertainty slithered in his gut.

"She's where she belongs. That's all that matters." He watched the patrol car roll past the storage facility gate and turn down the road out of sight. "Madison confirmed Rosalind used Harvey Braddock as a messenger between her and Pierce Cook until the defense attorney learned they planned to kill her. Can we tie his death to either of them?"

A heavy sigh escaped from Remi's mouth. Out of exhaustion or defeat, he wasn't sure. He'd never seen his deputy chief so…burdened. "The thermite burned any kind of DNA evidence left behind. The medical examiner only had so much to work with, but cause of death was narrowed down to blunt-force trauma to the back of the head with a crowbar recovered at the scene. The fire made it impossible to match fingerprints to Cook. The ME will release the body so the family can claim him, but we can't charge a dead man with murder, and we can't prove Rosalind Eyler was involved. All we have her on is conspiracy."

"She's not talking." Jonah shook his head. The woman was going to spend the rest of her life behind bars for what they could prove against her. Why stop talking now?

"Not to us, but she seems to like you." Remi patted him on the shoulder, and he flinched against the pain from the shrapnel wound. "Sorry. Forgot you've already survived another bombing before today. Good work on this case, Watson. You saved a lot of people's lives. Can't imagine why the FBI let you get away."

"I left because of my son." Stillness swam through him as the past he'd been trying to hide surfaced. He waited for the shame, the anger, to rise, but facing the possibility of losing Madison and this new baby to forces outside his control had only hammered the truth deeper. Now there was only acceptance. Peace. Love. "I had a son before I quit the FBI. Noah. He would've been four now if he hadn't died."

Remi didn't answer, the weight of her attention fixed.

"There hadn't been anything I could do to save

him then. He passed away in his sleep while I was assigned overseas. I wasn't there for him, and I've had to deal with that guilt day in and day out ever since." Jonah shifted his gaze to his superior, and the emotional dam he'd built to protect himself from letting that same fear spread crumbled. "Madison's due in a few months, and I have no idea how to make sure it doesn't happen again."

"You can't," Remi said. She stared up at him as the sun climbed higher in the sky, blocking the brightness from her eyes with one hand. "You said it yourself. There was nothing you could do to save Noah, but that doesn't mean you weren't every bit the father he needed you to be. Maybe all you can do is be here for this baby and be here for Madison. They're the ones who need you now. Make every second count while you still have time."

A heaviness lifted from his chest as his deputy chief rejoined the officers going through what was left of evidence from the storage unit. Marshal Dylan Cove turned toward her as she approached, tracing his hand down her wrist, out of sight from the other officers around them, and Jonah smiled. Remi was right. Why worry about the past repeating itself when the present had so much more to offer? He'd always remember his first son. He'd always have those short few weeks between them. Because, if he was being honest, it'd been better than not having any time together at all. Jonah focused on the deputy district attorney who'd claimed his heart and stalked toward her.

The officer she'd been giving her statement to peeled off in another direction as Jonah slid one arm along Madison's lower back and spun her into him. The sling the EMTs had fit around her injured shoulder and wrist scraped along his clothing as she stared up at him, that perfect mouth parting in surprise. Her gaze assessed the personnel around them as she brushed a strand of hair out of her face, but he didn't care about who was watching. "Jonah—"

"I love you, Maddi. You're everything I've been missing in my life. You're the reason I keep taking escort details and lying about how good I am at crossword puzzles. You're on my mind when I wake up and the last person I think about when I go to sleep at night. You're the strongest, most independent woman I've ever had the pleasure of knowing, and I was an idiot to ask you to give up an entire piece of yourself for my own fear of losing you and the baby. I don't want to change you, and I don't need a commitment from you." Jonah lowered himself down onto one knee, her hand in both of his. "If you want to run for district attorney, I'll be the first one to cast my vote. If you want to support this baby on your own, I won't push your boundaries. I promise never to ask you to marry me or demand to be part of this baby's life. Because the choice is yours, Counselor. Whatever you're willing to give me, I'll take it, and I'll always be there for you."

Silence surrounded them, and Jonah realized the entire scene had come to a complete halt. Reed, Foster, Remington and Cove waited for her response, but Jonah could focus only on her.

A smile brightened Madison's face before she fell into his arms. She crushed her mouth to his, rocking him off balance, and wrapped her uninjured hand around the back of his neck. "Deal."

Three months later

JURY BENCHES HAD the potential to hide a lot of things, but Multnomah County District Attorney Madison Gray had attention only for the inmate on the other side of the courtroom.

Rosalind Eyler—the Rip City Bomber—had made it in once piece to the last day of her trial. Long bright red hair accentuated the lack of color in the woman's face, highlighted the shadows under her eyes. Her deal with Madison's predecessor had fallen through. There'd been no talks of another. Rosalind would spend the rest of her life behind bars without chance of parole. She hadn't personally triggered the bomb in the courtroom three months ago, but being charged as an accessory to Pierce Cook's crimes had brought the

grand total of bombing murder counts to forty-
one victims. All to be served consecutively. Her
new defense attorney, a young woman from Harvey Braddock's firm, hadn't even had a chance.

"The jury finds the defendant, Rosalind Eyler,
guilty. Bailiff, please take the defendant into custody so she can make the transport back to Corrections and serve out her days where she belongs.
This case is concluded." The judge slammed the
gavel on the base and rose. His dark robe shifted
around his feet as he stepped down from his seat
and disappeared into the corridor leading to his
chambers.

Madison struggled to her feet as murmurs
filled the courtroom. Turning to face the gallery,
she noted family members of the victims clasping hands, shedding tears and embracing, and the
heaviness she'd been burdened with since taking
on this case lifted. Forty-one victims, more injured
or disabled from the cruel acts of two killers. They
would have justice now.

It was over.

The Rip City Bomber wouldn't have the chance
to hurt anyone else.

Through the bustling of media and civilians as
the courtroom cleared, one face stood out among
the rest. A smile automatically curled Madison's
mouth wide as the deputy US marshal she'd fallen
in love with made his way through the sea of bodies.

"Congratulations, Counselor. You've just pros-ecuted the biggest criminal case in the state of Oregon." His deep voice penetrated through the buzz around them and filled her with warmth from head to toe. Bright blue eyes leveled with hers as he reached over the bar separating the gallery from the front of the courtroom and smoothed both hands over her nine-month-sized beach ball of a stomach. "Job's done."

"Marshal Watson, I thought I might find you here. How was the gravesite? Did you take the flowers I bought?" she asked.

"It was good." His shoulders deflated on a strong exhale. "I talked to him for a while, told him all about you and the little brother that will be here soon."

"Noah would've been a great big brother." Their son would make his grand entrance into the world any day now, but until then Madison would soak up every moment she could get with the man who'd kept his promise these past three months. No com-mitment. No custody and visitation agreement. Nothing to complicate or dissolve the connection they'd built since that day at the storage facility. She reached into her bag and pulled a folded piece of paper from the depths. Handing it to him, she memorized the way his eyebrows lifted slightly along his forehead. "I have something for you."

Pulling his hands back from her hips, he unfolded the piece of paper with a deep laugh rumbling through his chest. That gut-wrenching smile she couldn't get enough of outshone the jury's verdict against the Rip City Bomber. Almost. "A new crossword."

"When you got down on one knee, you said you were pretending you weren't good at them. I'd like to see you crack this one." She tapped the paper before she turned to collect her files from the table. A tightening in her belly washed through her, forcing her to hold her breath. Braxton-Hicks contractions. She'd gotten a few throughout the past couple of days, but that had definitely been the strongest of the set. "The reporters are champing at the bit downstairs. Care to escort me to the lobby?"

Jonah swung the gate open for her, the crossword in hand. The sooner he found the answers for every box, the sooner she'd have hers. "It would be my pleasure."

Side by side, they exited the newly refurbished courtroom. Memories ignited of the terrifying moments he'd carried her down this exact hallway after the bombing, but even then she'd known Jonah would do whatever it took to protect her and their son. He intertwined his hand with hers, but another contraction forced her to pull up short. Concern deepened the three lines between his eyebrows as she strengthened her grip around his hand. "Another Braxton-Hicks contraction?"

A flood of sensation pooled low between her legs as the contraction let up. That one had definitely been stronger than the one she'd experienced during court proceedings, and the interval had sped up. She pressed one hand into her left side and felt their son's movement underneath the thick lining of fat and muscle. "No, I don't think so."

"Maddi?" Jonah took position in front of her, framing the baby between both calloused hands. "Tell me what's going on."

"I'm fairly certain my water broke." She took a step forward and cringed against the trickling sensation running down the inside of her legs. "No, I'm definitely sure my water broke. Can you get me to my office, please? I have a change of clothes stashed in my overnight bag."

"We need to get you to the hospital." A combination of urgency and excitement transformed his expression as he took her bag from her shoulder and clasped both of her hands in his. "The baby's coming."

"No. Office first. I need to go to my office." She'd hold this baby in as long as it took. Although the next wave of tightening was already building. "This isn't the movies. Real life says I have at least a couple of hours before this baby shoots out of there."

"And you plan to have that happen in your office?" Clerks, attorneys and security personnel watched them as Jonah helped her shuffle toward the elevator.

"I'm not giving birth in my office, Jonah." She clamped her jaw against the oncoming squeeze from the top of her lungs to the bottom of her torso. Okay. They weren't going to make it to her office. She detoured to the nearest wall and slammed her hand down for something more solid to hold on to. "There's something I have to do first, but I'm pretty sure this watermelon isn't going to let me. Give…me my bag."

He did as she asked, confusion chasing back the excitement that'd been etched into his expression moments before. "What do you need?"

"A pen." An uncontrolled growl ripped up her throat as the third contraction in as many minutes constricted her midsection. "Or a pencil. That will work, too."

He dumped the contents of her bag onto the newly waxed tile and skimmed through everything inside until he'd found her a pen. "You're stopping in the middle of the courthouse corridor while you're in labor. This better be the best-damn-looking pen I've ever seen in my life."

"It's not for me." She had a break between contractions, and a flood of relief wrung the pain from her overtaxed muscles. "It's for you. You need to solve the crossword. Right now." A concerned security guard headed toward them, but Madison waved them off. "We're fine. I'm in labor. Not a big deal."

"You want me to solve the crossword now? Right this second?" Disbelief hiked his voice into the next octave. "You haven't even gotten to the hospital for the good drugs, and you're already hallucinating."

She left the safety of the wall and clenched his shirt in her hands as she dragged him into her. The physical pressure of their son working his way into the world was almost too much to take. They didn't have time for this. She knew that, but the part of her he'd saved that day at the storage facility needed him to do it. He'd kept his word all this time. He deserved to know how she really felt about him. "I will have this baby on the floor if I have to, Jonah. I need you to solve the damn crossword before we go to the hospital. I thought we'd have more time, but we don't. Understand?"

Jonah bit down on the end of the pen cap and pulled the pen free. "Fine. Three across." His mumblings grew fainter as he filled in the boxes as fast as he could, while Madison hung on to his shirt for dear life. Nervous energy skittered up her spine as Jonah's mouth parted. The pen cap bounced onto the floor and rolled away out of sight. He'd finished the puzzle. Her heart skipped a beat, and the pain faded as he raised that dependable gaze to hers. "Is this... Are you serious?"

"I've never been more serious about anything in my entire life. It took me weeks to put together." Madison nodded, reaching for his hand. She stared up at him. Her hair fell behind her shoulder as she prepared for the next contraction. "Deputy US Marshal Jonah Watson, you are the bravest, most loyal man and most dependable source of safety I've ever had at my side. I fell in love with you long before we made this baby together. You're the rock I've needed my entire life, my everything and the reason I'm standing here today. Before you rushed into my life, I was lost, but you helped me see there's more to a relationship—a marriage— than I ever imagined. I cut you out of my life after I found out I was pregnant, but I never want to spend another day apart again. I love you. So will you marry me?"

His smile slipped. "I promise you, you don't have to do this, Maddi. I'm happy being as involved in your life—in our son's life—as you want me to be. Whatever you need from me, it's yours."

"I need everything, Jonah. I need you. Now. Forever. You're everything I was scared of, and everything I've always dreamed of having, and I want to spend the rest of my life having these moments between us." She kissed him softly. "But if you could give me a quick answer, that would be great, because there's another contraction coming, and I might not remember this later."

His laugh vibrated through her and straight to her toes. "Yes."

"Yes?" Pure elation replaced the past few minutes of pain as he pressed his mouth to hers. Her feet left the ground as Jonah held her against him. She planted her hand against his chest as she settled on the four corners of her toes and smiled up at her marshal. Her life partner. Her everything. "Great. Now take me to the hospital. Noah's little brother isn't going to wait much longer."

Jonah hit her with that brilliant smile all over again and wrapped her hand in his. "You got it, Counselor."

* * * * *

WE HOPE YOU ENJOYED
THIS BOOK FROM

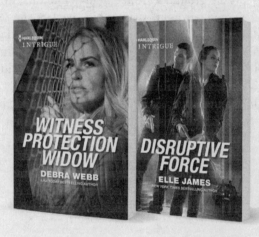

COMING NEXT MONTH FROM

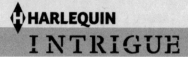

INTRIGUE

Available March 30, 2021

#1989 THE SECRET SHE KEPT
A Badge of Courage Novel • by Rita Herron
A disturbed student made Kate McKendrick's high school a hunting ground.
Now Kate's the school's principal, and she's working with former bad boy
Riggs Benford to uncover the secrets of that day and help the town heal.
But a vengeful individual will do anything to keep the truth hidden.

#1990 THE SETUP
A Kyra and Jake Investigation • by Carol Ericson
Detective Jake McAllister doesn't know Kyra Chase is connected to an
unsolved murder. He only knows his new case partner is a distraction. But
with the body count rising, they'll need to trust each other in order to catch a
killer who seems to know more about Kyra than Jake does.

#1991 PRESUMED DEADLY
The Ranger Brigade: Rocky Mountain Manhunt • by Cindi Myers
Dane Trask will do anything to bring down a drug ring, but he knows his first
step is getting Ranger Brigade officer Faith Martin's help. But when their
investigation means eluding Faith's fellow cops *and* an unknown killer, will
the rugged Colorado terrain help them...or ensure their demise?

#1992 THE SUSPECT
A Marshal Law Novel • by Nichole Severn
Remington Barton's failure to capture a murderer ruined her career as a
sheriff. Now she's a US marshal—and a suspect in a homicide. Her ex,
Deputy Marshal Dylan Cove, never stopped hunting for the killer who eluded
her. Can they prove her innocence before they become the next victims?

#1993 PROTECTING HIS WITNESS
Heartland Heroes • by Julie Anne Lindsey
When her safe house is breached, Maisy Daniels runs to Blaze Winchester,
the detective who didn't just investigate the murder of Maisy's sister. He's
also the father of her soon-to-be-born child. Can Blaze stop the killer hell-
bent on keeping Maisy from testifying?

#1994 K-9 COLD CASE
A K-9 Alaska Novel • by Elizabeth Heiter
With the help of his K-9 companion, FBI victim specialist Jax Diallo vows to
help police chief Keara Hernandez end the attacks against their community.
Evidence suggests the crimes are connected to her husband's unsolved
murder. When bullets fly, Jax will risk everything to keep his partner safe.

**YOU CAN FIND MORE INFORMATION ON UPCOMING HARLEQUIN TITLES,
FREE EXCERPTS AND MORE AT HARLEQUIN.COM.**

HICNM0321

He'd recognize that voice anywhere, even though he'd
heard it live and in person just a few times and never
so…forceful. He believed her, but he had no intention
of letting her off the hook so easily.

He raised his hands. "I'm LAPD Detective
Jake McAllister. Are you all right?"

A sudden gust of wind carried her sigh down the trail
toward him.

"It…it's Kyra Chase. I'm sorry. I'm putting away my
weapon."

Lowering his hands, he said, "Is it okay for me to
move now?"

"Of course. I didn't realize… I thought you were…"

"The killer coming back to his dump site?" He flicked on the flashlight in his hand and continued down the trail, his shoes scuffing over dirt and pebbles. "He wouldn't do that—at least not so soon after the kill."

When he got within two feet of her, he skimmed the beam over her body, her dark clothing swallowing up the light until it reached her blond hair. "I didn't mean to scare you, but what are you doing here?"

"Probably the same thing you are." She hung on to the strap of her purse, her hand inches from the gun pocket.

"I'm the lead detective on the case, and I'm doing some follow-up investigation."

"Believe it or not, Detective, I have my own prep work that I like to do before meeting a victim's family. I want to have as much information as possible when talking to them. I'm sure you can understand that."

"Sure, I can. And call me Jake."

Don't miss
The Setup *by Carol Ericson,*
available April 2021 wherever
Harlequin Intrigue books and ebooks are sold.

Harlequin.com

HIEXP0321

Get 4 FREE REWARDS!

We'll send you 2 FREE Books plus 2 FREE Mystery Gifts.

Harlequin Intrigue books are action-packed stories that will keep you on the edge of your seat. Solve the crime and deliver justice at all costs.

FREE
Value Over
$20

YES! Please send me 2 FREE Harlequin Intrigue novels and my 2 FREE gifts (gifts are worth about $10 retail). After receiving them, if I don't wish to receive any more books, I can return the shipping statement marked "cancel." If I don't cancel, I will receive 6 brand-new novels every month and be billed just $4.99 each for the regular-print edition or $5.99 each for the larger-print edition in the U.S., or $5.74 each for the regular-print edition or $6.49 each for the larger-print edition in Canada. That's a savings of at least 12% off the cover price! It's quite a bargain! Shipping and handling is just 50¢ per book in the U.S. and $1.25 per book in Canada.* I understand that accepting the 2 free books and gifts places me under no obligation to buy anything. I can always return a shipment and cancel at any time. The free books and gifts are mine to keep no matter what I decide.

Choose one: ☐ **Harlequin Intrigue Regular-Print**
(182/382 HDN GNXC)

☐ **Harlequin Intrigue Larger-Print**
(199/399 HDN GNXC)

Name (please print)

Address   Apt. #

City   State/Province   Zip/Postal Code

Email: Please check this box ☐ if you would like to receive newsletters and promotional emails from Harlequin Enterprises ULC and its affiliates. You can unsubscribe anytime.

> Mail to the **Harlequin Reader Service:**
> **IN U.S.A.:** P.O. Box 1341, Buffalo, NY 14240-8531
> **IN CANADA:** P.O. Box 603, Fort Erie, Ontario L2A 5X3

Want to try 2 free books from another series! Call 1-800-873-8635 or visit www.ReaderService.com.

*Terms and prices subject to change without notice. Prices do not include sales taxes, which will be charged (if applicable) based on your state or country of residence. Canadian residents will be charged applicable taxes. Offer not valid in Quebec. This offer is limited to one order per household. Books received may not be as shown. Not valid for current subscribers to Harlequin Intrigue books. All orders subject to approval. Credit or debit balances in a customer's account(s) may be offset by any other outstanding balance owed by or to the customer. Please allow 4 to 6 weeks for delivery. Offer available while quantities last.

Your Privacy—Your information is being collected by Harlequin Enterprises ULC, operating as Harlequin Reader Service. For a complete summary of the information we collect, how we use this information and to whom it is disclosed, please visit our privacy notice located at corporate.harlequin.com/privacy-notice. From time to time we may also exchange your personal information with reputable third parties. If you wish to opt out of this sharing of your personal information, please visit readerservice.com/consumerschoice or call 1-800-873-8635. **Notice to California Residents**—Under California law, you have specific rights to control and access your data. For more information on these rights and how to exercise them, visit corporate.harlequin.com/california-privacy.

HI21R